A
SEASON
FOR
GHOSTS

RICHARD M PEARSON

'A Season for Ghosts' is the fourth book by Richard M Pearson.

I started this journey with the release of my first novel, 'The Path' in 2018. I initially planned it to be a one-off, but life has a habit of taking you down a different road to the one you expect. There is a saying that everybody has one book to write and that was supposed to be mine. After some lovely feedback and positive reviews, I decided to do a follow up called, 'Deadwater.' From that point on I seemed to get a small but loyal cult following who encouraged me to keep writing. Every time I finish a new book, I feel it may be my last, who knows. All I can say is that writing has proven to be a journey with many twists and turns, just like my books I suppose. In fact, just like life.

I was born in England and then lived in Wales and Northern Ireland before finally landing in Bonnie Scotland at the impressionable age of eight. You could call me multi-cultural but in a homely sort of way. My stories tend to be based in Scotland, a country I have a deep passion for. Having said that, travel does make the heart grow fonder so I will occasionally take you to other dark and distant lands.

Reading has always been one of my great passions. I love books that build up a gothic atmosphere of foreboding, the first half of Dracula by Bram Stoker being a classic example. In my opinion, a good book should always have an unexpected finale. I will never forget reading 'Rebecca' by Daphne Du Maurier and the way the twist turned the whole story on its head.

I hope that by the time you have finished this book you will have enjoyed the journey into the dark corners of your imagination. As I mentioned before, we all have the potential to write a book. Maybe mine will inspire you to give it a go as well.

More information available at
rmpearson.net

I am never sure if she enjoys my dark tales of ghosts and the macabre. Despite this, every new page is given the same quiet attention until I am finished reading it to her. Little will be said but I will know immediately if my story has worked or not. This book is dedicated to you, Wee Mo, because you listen to me. What more could I ask as a writer?

In memory of our dear friend, Sam (1959-2019)

A SEASON FOR
GHOSTS CONTENTS

Introduction

Do you believe in ghosts? I do and yet I must be one of the most cynical people you could meet when it comes to accepting something I cannot physically see or touch. Maybe it is the same for all and until the vision presents itself in front of us, we doubt it can be real. But trust me on this one, even if you do not believe right now, one day you will. It is only a matter of time before the spirits come to meet you. You might even have to die first, but hopefully not.

Until a few weeks ago I was simply a pedlar of fiction, ghost fiction. It stirred my imagination to write books about the macabre and the weird. As you will read later on, things changed dramatically for me when I met the tall man. Now that I have found my ghost, I feel different. Maybe I write my stories with more respect. Could it be possible that I now have a real sense of foreboding and fear? Have I suddenly changed from writing fiction to documenting real facts? There is so much that we human beings do not understand. Who the hell are we and what are we doing on this floating planet stuck in the middle of a vast universe?

How could anyone doubt that ghosts exist when we know so little about who or what we really are.

I hope you will enjoy the journey you are about to embark on. This book contains nine separate short stories and four seasonal interludes. You will find yourself trapped in the snow at a lonely railway station, stuck on a flight with some weird cabin crew, go on strange blind dates, meet the ghost of the quarry, walk 800 miles to the land of the shadows and help an alcoholic lord find the weirdest Christmas present ever. Hopefully, these dark tales of the strange and the macabre will keep you so engrossed that you will forget to look over your shoulder as the deep night descends around you. But don't worry, if you miss meeting your ghost this time, it will be sure to come back. I for one know that I have not seen the last of the Tall man.

SEA SHADOW

I never believe people when they say, *Oh I really enjoy flying.* This usually comes just after you have mentioned how much you hate it. I mean, who in their right mind would seriously like flying? You wait in endless queues at the airport, ticket check, baggage check, passport check, security check. In between each of these, you get to sit around for hours while constantly looking at the departure board. When they announce, 'Go to gate 372', everyone charges forward simply to stand in another queue while people with special tickets or wheelchairs brush past you with an air of superiority. And after you have gone through all this? Well, then you get to sit crushed up in a flimsy-looking tin tube with wings while a smiling uniformed trolley dolly peddles you overpriced food and drink. But that is not the end of it. No sir, after all that hell, you then get to spend the next endless hours waiting for a wing to fall off or an engine to catch fire and take you to certain death in the ocean below. Let's be clear on one thing, there are two kinds of passengers on a plane, those that hate flying and those that also hate flying.

Now, having said all that, I personally don't mind flying, but Lachlan Jarvie hated everything about it, with a passion. You would have thought that having spent so much time floating in the clouds his mood would have improved over the years. Not a bit of it. Every time his job sent him on another trip across the sea, he would feel the tension rising from the minute the taxi picked him up and headed towards Glasgow Airport. But this time there was a silver lining. In exactly one week he would be taking early retirement, getting the fuck out of the rat race, becoming a man of leisure. So why did he feel even more agitated and tense this time, probably his last ever forced flight? Maybe that was it, the pent-up frustration and anger from the hundreds of previous flights was ready to explode. Maybe this one last journey was going to be his big act of revenge.

'You going on holiday then?' The cab driver spoke the words into one of those crackly taxi intercoms. The type that makes it sound like your driver is an alien from Uranus. He might as well be on Uranus because the electronic voice is almost inaudible.

Why is it that when we mention the planets, as soon

as someone says Uranus, we all start laughing? Well, I do anyway, I giggle like a two-year-old. Most men do, women don't laugh at the mention of Uranus, they are a bit more mature I suppose.

Lachlan looked down at the neatly pressed suit he was wearing and then his leather briefcase before responding in a world-weary tone.

'Yes, I am going to Benidorm, just me, the wife and our six kids.' The taxi driver looked at him through the rear-view mirror. He was a big guy, Glaswegian big, the kind you don't act smart with. Not unless you fancy playing handball with your teeth. Lachlan feared his sarcasm had overstepped the mark; it would not be the first time. Another few seconds passed before Mr. Big in the front seat replied.

'Ma wife loves Benidorm. I do too, you should take the kids to The Rangers bar, fucking great place. All decked out in red, white and blue and only two fucking euros a beer. Tennent's as well, none of that Spanish muck.'

Now, look. Before I continue with this story, let me add in a wee disclaimer. (Wee means small in Scotland. In England, it is used to describe the liquid stuff you deposit in a Toilet. I am not sure what it means in America or Nigeria.) Anyway, back to the disclaimer. The comment about The

Rangers Bar from the Big Man could just as easily be turned into,

'Ma wife loves Benidorm. I do too, you should take the kids to The Celtic bar, fucking great place. All decked out in green and white and only two fucking euros a beer. Tennent's as well, none of that Spanish muck.' Most of you will be wondering what on earth I am talking about but trust me on this one. If you live in Glasgow like me, then it is ok to make jokes about both sides of the footballing divide but never about one on its own. Not unless you want both the Celtic Big Man and the Rangers Big Man to re-arrange your legs so that they fit into your ears.

Lachlan was seated in the departure lounge. He smiled to himself, it was time to calm down. The sensible voice in his head had given him a dressing down. *This will be your last journey, the final trip before you call it a day. Why not enjoy it, don't get into any arguments, smile at everyone and they will smile with you.* It was the sort of lecture his wife usually gave him. *One of these days you will have a heart attack, getting yourself into such a state over nothing.* This time he was going to listen, the angry voice in his head had gone to bed. The sensible voice was in charge. Lachlan had even kept his cool going through security. 'Laptops in a separate tray, Sir.'

'Ok, no problem.'

'You will need to remove both shoes, Sir.'

'Ok, no problem.'

'Can you remove the belt on your trousers, Sir.'

'Ok, no problem.'

'Can you place any loose change and metal objects in the tray, Sir.'

'Ok, no problem.'

'Can I ask you to remove your head and stick it up your arse, Sir.'

'Ok, no problem.'

It was warm in the departure lounge, despite the air conditioning. Summer had been unusually hot in Glasgow. In fact, the word hot and Glasgow rarely go together. Baltic, freezing, wet, cold, fucking miserable, pissing with rain, bucketing down, these are Glaswegian words. Hot is kept for visits to Benidorm or Majorca on holiday. Lachlan glanced at the screen hanging from the ceiling, flight DCM623 for Valencia continued to state, wait in the departure lounge. He knew it was going to be late taking off. It was now 9:15 and it was scheduled to leave at 9:50. *No chance we are leaving at 9:50, oh well Lachlan old boy. Who cares, this is the last one. I shall never have to fly again, holidays at home from now on.*

Lachlan never had alcohol when he was travelling on business. As he sat waiting, the sensible voice started talking to him. *The meeting is not until tomorrow, why not have a little glass of wine, make this last journey a celebration.* Now before you get confused and wonder if I am getting the sensible voice and the angry voice mixed up, let me explain. Sensible knew that one glass of wine would calm Lachlan down, keep him from getting agitated and then annoyed. The angry voice would always be hovering in the background ready to take over.

The young woman at the bar had perfected the act of looking completely disinterested in whatever she was doing. She poured the large white wine into the glass and placed it on the bar close to the till. It meant Lachlan had to take a few steps to retrieve his prize. 'Twelve pounds eighty.' She spoke the words without even looking at him.

Twelve fucking pounds eighty, I wanted a glass, not the fucking bottle. He felt like emptying the wine over her head but instead, he smiled and handed over two notes, ten pounds, and five pounds.

'Thank you, keep the change. This is my last trip before I retire, I don't usually drink at nine in the morning.' He felt his face redden as the young woman took the money and ignored him. Within seconds she had moved onto the next victim, I mean customer.

He sipped his wine slowly while scanning the lounge. When you have spent so much of your life waiting in airports, you get to read the signs that others will miss. Two pilots and three attendants walked with assurance amongst the throng. They could have been for any of the innumerable flights leaving that morning but somehow, he knew they were the flight crew for his plane. The two male pilots wore blue suits with caps, the two females and one male crew following behind in a mixture of grey and red. Maybe it was the wine kicking in, but Lachlan could not help thinking that they looked like human fish. Pointed stern faces moving in perfect unison across the floor. He smiled with an air of superiority when the screen above immediately changed to, Flight DCM623, go to gate 17A. Lachlan emptied the large wine and stood up. *Time to join the fish faces and another queue.*

It was all going ok until the line of passengers walking down the tunnel came to a sudden stop. From then on it was one step every few minutes. Ahead of him, Lachlan could see fraught conversations taking place between those at the front of the queue and the air hostesses.

Even as I typed that last sentence, I could sense that I was overstepping the boundary with regard to being PC correct. You are no longer allowed to call them air hostesses as that implies, they are female and of course, you now get male air hostesses. You also get nonbinary hostesses, so that makes getting the correct words even more complicated. Calling them Air hostesses is better than using the word trolley dolly but to keep up with the times, they are now known as cabin crew. Personally, I just say, *excuse me*. That negates any reason to get into a conversation regarding the correct usage of titles for airline staff. One last bit of advice, do not click your fingers and shout, *hey darlin*, is the bar open yet? They don't like that, not one bit.

'But I always bring this bag onboard, it has never been a problem in the past.' Lachlan spoke the words calmly and even tried to smile. The woman standing in the doorway of the plane was obviously the head steward. Her cold eyes stared back at him, her face rigid with a lack of emotion. The lips of her large mouth parted in readiness to reply. The angry voice in his head was talking to him, *she really does look like a fish. Maybe a Cod or a Sea Bass. A trout at best, but an ugly one.*

'What you did on other flights has no impact on what

is required on this one, Sir. I will have to have your bag placed in the hold if you want to come onboard.'

Tell fish face to fuck off, go on I dare you. Lachlan ignored the voice and smiled at the fish woman.

'Ok, would it be all right If I just take my laptop and a few things out first?'

'Sir, you are holding up the rest of the passengers. You can remove whatever you want but you will need to go back to the end of the queue.' He could tell that she did not like him. Maybe she could read his mind and was taking exception to being likened to a fish, even though she did look like a Sea Bass.

Lachlan was the last one to struggle to his seat. His ticket was for 58A, the window seat, but a large man was already occupying it. He turned and smiled.

'Oh sorry, I just assumed that this one was empty. I have the aisle seat; do you want me to move?' It was obvious that he did not expect to be asked to follow up on his offer. The man was big, the folds of his sides spilling over into the unoccupied middle seat. *Go on, tell the big lump to move. The bloody plane will tip over if he stays beside the window.* Again, Lachlan ignored the angry voice and smiled at the man.

'No problem at all. I prefer an aisle seat anyway.' He

was lying of course but still sticking to the promise he had made to himself. *Keep calm and smile, this is the last ever journey.*

'Good morning, this is Captain Joseph Coral welcoming you onboard flight DCM623 to Valencia. We will shortly be taxying to the runway once we get final clearance from control. We apologise for the late take off this morning. This was due to a broken-down fuelling truck at Glasgow airport. Hopefully, we can make up some time when we get in the air. Once we take off, we will circle the West coast of Scotland to gain height before heading across to Ireland and then turning south towards the coast of France. Please relax and enjoy the excellent hospitality onboard, including food, drink and scratch cards. You will be in the capable hands of our chief steward, Melanie Bream this morning. If you have any questions, she will be only too delighted to help you.'

Is it just me that gets annoyed when the Pilot comes on and says things like, *we shall head West for twenty minutes before turning East towards our destination?* Why not just go East from the start? The other thing is, does anyone care if we are flying over the tip of Ireland or floating over Greenland, we just want to get to our destination, alive preferably. Shut the fuck up and get on with keeping this flying coffin in the air. Thank you.

No one was listening to Captain Coral or watching Miss Bream as she went through the safety charade and pointed to the emergency exit doors. Why would you be worried about an exit door if you crashed into the Atlantic? I am no, flight accident investigator but I reckon neither you nor the door would be around to do any exiting after you collide with the ocean at 500 miles an hour.

In the seat opposite was a young woman with a child. The boy was probably around six and Lachlan already knew his name. 'Scott, will you sit in your seat, you need to keep your seatbelt on like mummy is doing.' This was just the invite little Scott needed to start taking his seatbelt off.

'Scott, will you keep your feet still, you are kicking mummy.'

'Scott, stop that or no games on the tablet.'

'Scott, I told you before, put that seatbelt back on or mummy will get angry.' All this was said in the same monotone voice. Pointless words simply spoken to let the other passengers know that she was a good parent. Everyone else knew that the little runt was the one in charge.

Why don't you jump over to his seat and kick the little shit in the nuts? Lachlan smiled at the thought but of course, he ignored the angry voice. He leaned over to the young woman and offered some words of encouragement.

'Don't worry, we have all been there. My two were the same. They are not much better now, and they are both in their twenties.' The woman smiled at him and nodded her appreciation for his support. Little Scott looked at him with scorn in his eyes. The child's voice in his head was probably saying, *what the fuck has it got to do with you, you interfering old git. One more smart comment from you and you might end up with a kick in the nuts.* The voice probably didn't say that, it would have been good though.

Lachlan decided to have another large wine. Unfortunately, it was going to be a bit of a wait. The male cabin person was moving his trolley slowly up the aisle. His crablike arms constantly shooting back and forth as he supplied the passengers with food and drinks. Before I move on with my story, can I just take some credit for that opening sentence? Did you notice I called the male Trolley Dolly a cabin person? That shows how PC correct I can be when I make the effort. You can thank me later.

'Can I have a large white wine please?' The Crab looked down at Lachlan as though he was some sort of alcoholic.

'This is my last flight before I retire, been doing this

route for the last twenty years. I thought I might just have a little celebration.'

'We don't have large white wines, Sir. Do you want two small bottles?' Crab said the words while looking through Lachlan as though he was invisible.

'That would be fine, Yes, why not. Two small bottles then. I bet you would love to have a little drink as well. You guys work so hard on these flights.'

'That will be fifteen pounds, Sir.'

They were already a few hours into the flight. Lachlan felt good, the wine was giving him that warm hazy feeling. The phase between sobriety and being drunk. I like to think that is the best bit. Stop at that point and you are hangover free the following day. I don't tend to stop at that bit though, so I can't vouch for my observation being entirely correct.

Little Scott was now swinging his legs backward and forward, kicking the seat in front of him. Luckily it was empty. As Lachlan sipped his wine it suddenly dawned on him that the flight was barely half full. This was extremely unusual but a bonus as far as he was concerned. I tend to like the sight of empty seats on a flight. Less weight to carry, smaller chance of falling out of the sky. No doubt some scientist has a graph that shows fully laden flights are safer, but I still feel better when there are empty seats. Anyway, it means you can get wine and scratch cards from the trolley dolly quicker. Sorry, I mean cabin person, male, female or non-binary.

'I need to go to the toilet mummy; I need to go to the toilet mummy. I need to go ….' The child's irate mother was already unfastening his seat belt. Lachlan hoped she was going to strangle him with it, but he was already bouncing out of the chair.

'Go in that one, just behind us. No messing around or you will get into trouble Scott.' The little boy skipped off towards the lavatory at the rear of the plane. Lachlan sank back in his seat to enjoy a few minutes of peace and quiet. His hand went to pick up the plastic tumbler of wine. He expected it to be heavier and was disappointed to see he had already polished off most of the two little bottles. *Should I get some more wine? Why not, after all, this is my last trip, the final journey.* You may have guessed by now that the encouragement to buy another drink was coming from the angry voice. The sensible voice had packed up for the day and gone to bed. Lachlan looked down the aisle to see if Crab was around but unfortunately, Melanie Bream was now pushing the trolley. She stood talking to one of the passengers at the front of the plane.

'Would you mind keeping an eye on my stuff? I think that little rogue should be back from the bathroom by now.' The woman's voice made him jump in his seat.

'Of course, I will.' The young mother smiled at him and then edged her way towards the toilet to extricate young Scott from whatever mischief he had got involved in.

Lachlan sat for the next ten minutes watching the slow progress of Miss Bream as she smiled and chatted with the passengers. Somehow, he knew that when she arrived at his seat, the smile would be replaced by contempt, even more so when he asked her for another two little bottles of wine. Bream finally arrived next to him, she made to walk past without looking. 'Excuse me.'

'Yes Sir, how may I help?' She said the words while looking over his head, almost as though she preferred talking to the window rather than him.

'Could I have another two bottles of wine, if that's ok?' This time her cold fish-like eyes looked down to focus on him.

'I have stopped serving for now.' Even as she said the words, she bent down to lift two bottles and another plastic tumbler before placing them abruptly on the tray in front of Lachlan.

'Oh, it is ok, I can just use the tumbler I have. We should do our wee bit to save the planet, eh?' She ignored his feeble attempt at humour.

'That will be fifteen pounds Sir, and if you don't mind me saying, I think that should be your last alcoholic drink. We have strict rules for unruly passengers onboard our flights.' She marched away quickly before the shocked Lachlan could respond.

Lachlan was furious. *How dare she infer that I am drunk. Bloody hell what is wrong with that fish-faced woman? I have been polite and only had a few drinks and yet she accuses me of being unruly.* It was only then that it dawned on him that the young woman had been away for more than fifteen minutes. It seemed odd; he could see the toilet as it was only a few rows behind him. Only one other passenger occupied a seat further down the cabin than Lachlan. She looked like a middle-aged schoolteacher. A frumpy tweed skirt and reading glasses perched on the end of her nose as she read her book. He waited another ten minutes while he polished off one of the little bottles and then decided to go and investigate. Miss School teacher ignored his shaky progress as he edged towards the rear of the plane. The toilet door was slightly open. He pushed it slowly, not sure what to expect. The lavatory was empty. On his way back to his seat he stopped beside the woman and bent down to attract her attention. 'Excuse me, did you see where the young woman and child went to? They walked passed you about 30 minutes ago?' She placed the book on her lap and slowly removed her reading glasses.

'I have no idea what you are talking about and if you don't return to your seat, I am going to get the steward and tell her you are harassing me.'

Lachlan was back in his seat with the large man snoring beside him. He was confused and was now beginning to doubt himself. *This is so weird. Why was that old cow so rude to me? I asked her politely. Jeez, she is as bad as the cabin crew on this plane.* He tried to rationalise what had occurred but no matter how much he thought it through, the simple fact was that the young woman and child had disappeared. *Had they passed him and gone to sit at the front of the plane? After all, there were plenty of empty seats.* And yet he would have seen them going past. The only logical explanation he could come up with was that the wine was getting him tipsy and the missing woman was indeed now sitting in another row with little Scott.

Lachlan pushed the last unopened small bottle away and watched as Crab edged his way down the aisle towards him. 'Excuse me, would you mind…?' The young man stopped and gave him a cold stare, his crab-like arms swinging at his side. He spoke abruptly before Lachlan could finish his question.

'I am sorry Sir, but I have been instructed by Head Steward Bream that we are not to sell any more alcohol to you.'

'No, no, I don't want any more wine, thank you. I was just wondering where the young woman and child sitting over there had moved to?' He pointed at the empty seats as he spoke. Crab turned and glanced before reverting his cold gaze at Lachlan.

'Sir, I will have to ask you to calm down, you may upset the other passengers. If you continue to cause problems, we will have to call ahead for Police assistance when we land in Valencia.' Crab glared down at him, his eyes blue as the ocean.

'Do I make myself clear, Sir?' Lachlan stared back at him completely stunned.

'Yes, yes, quite clear. I am sorry; it was just that…' Crab was already walking away.

Lachlan sat in his seat with his brain in a whirl. *What the hell was going on? Why was everyone being so rude to him and what had happened to the young woman and her annoying kid?* The cabin of a plane made him feel claustrophobic at the best of times. Now he felt under siege from both the aircraft and the crew. There was nothing else for it. *Sit quietly and say nothing, get the hell off this flight. Maybe I just need a good sleep. Yes, that's it, get a good rest when I arrive at the hotel and all this will make sense tomorrow.*

Someone touched his left arm and Lachlan jumped in shock. It was the big man, the one who had slept beside him for most of the flight so far. His smiling jowly face was staring at him. Damp sweat gave the lines on his forehead a light sheen in the bright cabin lighting. 'Have I missed the drinks, bugger. I always fall asleep at the start of a flight.' Lachlan smiled back at him; it was nice to hear a friendly voice after his run-in with Crab.

'Yes, unfortunately, you have.' He leaned closer to his fellow passenger and lowered his voice.

'If I was you, I would not ask any of the fish-faced crew on this fucking plane for a drink, they will probably have you arrested.' The big man laughed at what he assumed was a joke. Lachlan pushed his last little bottle of wine towards his new accomplice.

'You can have that bottle if you want. According to the fish people, I have already had too much.' The big man was unbuckling his seatbelt.

'That is very kind of you, I might take you up on that offer. My mouth feels like Robert the Bruce is using it for a cave at the moment. I need to drain the radiator first though.' With that final comment, he pointed his large bulk at the toilet and staggered towards it. Lachlan watched him close the door before shouting,

'Let me know if you find a young woman and a child hiding in there?' Before he could even smile at his own joke Lachlan could see a member of the cabin crew moving swiftly down the aisle towards him. It was the final one of the three, the only one he had yet to fall out with. *Oh fuck, here comes another member of the fish family and this one is so skinny she looks like a finger. A fish finger, that is.* The angry voice in his head was goading him into a fight but he battled against the temptation even though the sensible voice was still in hiding.

'Sir, I really must ask you to stop shouting. You have already been warned about your behaviour by Miss Bream and crew member Julian Dredger. Why are you shouting?'

Lachlan took a deep breath and tried to speak in as low a voice as possible.

'I was just trying to show my fellow passenger where the toilet was, that is all.' Finger looked at him as though he had only recently escaped from a lunatic unit.

'Fellow passenger, what on earth are you talking about?' As Lachlan stared at her in confusion, he could make out the shape of Miss Bream hurrying down the aisle to join in the fracas.

'The big man, he has just gone into the lavatory, go and look if you don't believe me. What on earth is wrong with you people?' Melanie Bream was now standing beside her colleague Fish Finger.

'Is there a problem here Miss Saltwater?' Lachlan was becoming more and more confused.

'I thought your name was Miss Fish Finger. Who is Miss Saltwater?' The two women looked at each other with a worried expression.

'This is the final straw. Sir, I must ask you to stop shouting and making a commotion. We have already reported you to the Police at Valencia airport. If you don't calm down, we will have to ask the captain to put you in restraints. We have no choice as you are upsetting the other passengers with your aggressive behaviour.' Lachlan pointed to the toilet.

'Look if you don't believe me go and check. Try the toilet door, you will find it is locked because the big feller is in there.' What followed could have been a comedy routine from a television show. Lachlan had no sooner said the words than the Tweed covered schoolteacher placed her book down and took off her reading glasses. She looked over at the commotion and shook her head. Slowly she stood up and squeezed out of her seat. She turned right and walked towards the toilet door. Her hand grabbed the handle and just before disappearing, she turned and spoke.

'That man is a drunken lunatic. No one has been to this lavatory since the flight took off.' She closed the door behind her. Lachlan turned around to face Bream and Finger and was shocked to see that Crab was now running down the aisle towards the ensemble closely followed by Captain Coral. Lachlan finally broke, he had had enough of this weirdness. *Why were they picking on him, he had done nothing wrong? He was just trying to be a good citizen, showing concern for his fellow passengers who seemed to be disappearing in the cabin toilet.* The angry voice was now in full command. The sensible voice had woken up with a shock and attempted to intervene, but it was far too late. Lachlan jumped a few steps back and faced up to the group of crew members now descending on him.

'Look here, you fucking bunch of fish-faced losers. Why don't the fucking lot of you go and take a swim in the ocean with the rest of the fucking dolphins.' The words had hardly left his mouth before Captain Coral and Crab had him pinned to the floor. Bream was pulling a roll of tape with her teeth and stretching it out. Finger tried to block the view so that the other passengers upfront could not see what was going on.

'What the fuck are you doing you fucking bunch of squids, you will all be sacked for th...' Bream placed the tape over his mouth and within seconds they had bound his hands and feet with the rest of the roll. They carried the stunned and struggling Lachlan to the empty rear seat beside the toilet and roughly placed him in a sitting position. The crew dusted themselves down and headed off to placate the rest of the passengers leaving Captain Coral to administer the lecture.

Would you mind if I just break off the story here for a few seconds to make an observation? Have you ever been on a plane in mid-flight and seen the pilot standing talking to the cabin crew upfront? I have. Look, I know that they have computers and maybe even robots to fly the planes but come on. Let's imagine you are on your laptop booking a holiday. If there was an option that said, Flight, manned by person or robot? Who the hell would seriously tick, oh, Robot, please? I will bet you right at this minute that every single passenger who witnessed the Captain chatting up the female cabin crew on the flight I mentioned was thinking exactly the same as me. *Oh, for fuck sake, we are all going to die.*

Captain Coral gave the bound Lachlan a speech letting him know that he was in serious trouble and would be arrested on his arrival in Valencia. He wanted to punch the suited prick in the mouth but the only thing he could move at the moment was his head. He watched him walk back down to the front of the plane. They had drawn a curtain across the divide between the last three rows and the rest of the cabin. Lachlan could see the seat he had been sitting in just in front of him. The last little full bottle of wine stood taunting him. So near and yet so far.

Suddenly the frumpy tweed schoolteacher re-appeared from the toilet. Lachlan wanted to congratulate her on being the only person to survive a visit to the lavatory. Of course, he could say nothing but stare at her. She sat down in the empty seats opposite him. This in itself was odd, *why would they not have told her to move to the front if he was as dangerous as they seemed to think*. This whole trip had been so bizarre that Lachlan was no longer surprised at what was happening. He was resigned to the fact that he was in trouble. *He would fight his case though; he had done nothing wrong. The crew seemed to overreact to everything he did.*

Tweed was looking at him, a grin spreading across her squashy lined face. 'I could remove that tape across your mouth but how can I be sure you won't start shouting or even try to bite me?'

The tape meant that Lachlan had to breathe through his nose. He always had nasal problems caused by the air conditioning when he flew. He was desperate to have the gag removed and his eyes pleaded with Tweed to help him. She leaned over towards him and held out her hairy hand. 'My name is Laura Trawler although I prefer to use my maiden name, Laura Sinkbottom. Yes, you can call me Mrs. Sinkbottom if you like.' She laughed and pulled her hand back.

'Oh, I am such a silly billy. You can't shake my hand, can you? No of course not, you are all tied up like a Salmon in a net.' She laughed again. Lachlan's eyes pleaded with her for mercy. He tried desperately to free his arms from the tape that held them tight against his torso.

'I don't think you should struggle. I mean you have been a very angry and tiresome little man. If I was you, I would accept my fate. You don't want to upset the staff on the plane any more than you already have.' As he watched her something was beginning to dawn on him. It was her facial features, they had similar contours and lines to the others. *Yes, that was it, Laura Trawler or Sinkbottom as she was now called, Captain Coral, Melanie Bream, Crab and Fish Finger, they all had the same look, they all reminded him of the sea.* To be more precise, they reminded him of creatures from the sea.

She leaned over towards his seat and slowly removed the tape from around his mouth. 'You had better behave yourself you horrible little man or I will have to put the gag back on.' The feeling of relief washed over Lachlan. He was able to breathe, speak, be a free human being again. Well free to an extent, his body was still taped together.

'I, I won't cause any problems, Tweed, I mean Sinkbottom. Could I ask you to do me one little favour, please?' She looked at him and answered in a tone that mocked. Almost as if she was a fish just about to swallow the humblest of plankton.

'It depends what it is you want, I suppose. You feeble excuse for a human being.' He ignored her insults and kept calm.

'Would it be possible for you to let me have a drink of that last little bottle of wine on the seat in front of us. My mouth is so dry after wearing that gag, I am absolutely parched.' She stood up and reached over to place the little bottle into her hands. Slowly she edged towards her prisoner while her hairy hands screwed the top off. Lachlan leaned forward and opened his mouth, his tongue extended to accept the liquid. Laura Sinkbottom went to tip it into his mouth and then with a gargled laugh she emptied the full contents down her own throat as she stood in front of him.

It was the final straw. With every ounce of his strength, he pulled his legs apart and the tape ripped, freeing the bottom half of his body. Tweed stood transfixed in horror as Lachlan's left leg swung back and made perfect contact with her crotch. The kick sent her flying backward over the seat behind. The wine spraying out of her mouth as she sailed through the air. She let out a massive scream as her body disappeared although the tops of her legs protruded above row 57.

Lachlan knew the game was up now for sure. He hopped to his feet and with his arms still bound he headed for the toilet. He could already hear the clatter of shoes as the crew came running down the aisle. Within seconds he had made it through the door and kicked it closed, his eyes shut tightly in concentration. He turned his back to it and despite his hands being taped close together, Lachlan managed to manoeuvre his fingers around the lock and pull it over. Outside the door, he could hear the crew shouting as they tried to retrieve Laura Sinkbottom from the floor of the plane. Lachlan placed his ear to the door, waiting for the inevitable demands for him to open it. But nothing happened, incredibly it went quiet outside. *What the hell are they up to now?*

It was the silence that brought his attention back to the inside of the lavatory. A tiny room with a toilet and a sink. He wondered how on earth the big man who had slept beside him had even managed to get through the door. Lachlan looked for something he could use to free his arms from the tape. It was hopeless, the room offered nothing but the cramped ability to allow humans to discharge their waste. He kicked the toilet seat lid and sat down to think what his next move should be. *What an absolute fucking mess you have got yourself into this time old boy.* Suddenly the light started to flicker, and the crackly voice of Captain Coral floated out of the tiny speaker in the roof of the bathroom.

"This is your Captain speaking, just to give you an update on our progress. We are currently heading over the South coast of France at an altitude of 34,000 feet. Winds are moderate and we are well on schedule to arrive in Valencia on time. I hope you have enjoyed the flight. The temperature in Valencia is around 28-29 degrees, just slightly warmer than Glasgow. I will update you further once we start our descent. Until then, why don't you sit back, relax and take advantage of some of the excellent duty-free bargains available from our cabin staff."

Lachlan could not understand it. The Captain sounded so normal and calm. *Surely the rest of the plane had seen and heard the commotion. What the hell was going on and what had happened to the missing passengers? Had he imagined it, surely not? Am I going crazy?*

Lachlan scanned the tiny room, his brain trying to make sense of it all. *They had come in here, no matter what tweed and the rest of the fish family said, he had seen it happen with his own two eyes.* Lachlan felt his seated body jump in fright as the intercom crackled back to life.

'This is your Captain speaking. To you Mr. Lachlan Jarvie.' The smooth tone had gone to be replaced by a slithery meanness.

'I just want to say goodbye, the whole crew wants to wish you a safe final journey, you awful little man. Say goodbye everyone, say cheerio to the man in the toilet.' He could hear the rest of the fish family all shout their farewell in unison. Lachlan screamed at the top of his voice.

'You will all pay for this when we get to the airport. This is fucking outrageous you bunch of nutcases. I will be reporting every last one of you, just you wait and see. This will be the last flight you lot will ever be allowed to do.' Even if anyone could hear him, his ranting was being ignored. The voice on the intercom changed to Melanie Bream, a slimy velvet tone of hatred.

'Oh, we almost forgot. Before you leave us, I have to change your name. The Sea shadows will not accept an ugly little man called Lachlan Jarvie. No, from this point on you shall be known as Lachlan Driftwood. A fitting name don't you think?' He stood up and tried to make one final attempt to free his arms, his anger rising at the cruel taunts emanating from the little speaker. They were chanting now, weird nonsense. He tried to ignore it as he desperately twisted and turned in the vain hope, he could free himself from the tape. He wanted to unlock the door and go down fighting, take them all on.

We give our Sea shadow this offering. We send you our sacrifice Mr. Lachlan Driftwood. We give this man thing to the ocean. Accept our gift for free passage across your blue vastness. Take this human offering from your one true family.

Something was happening with his feet. Why was he moving without having to do anything? Lachlan's eyes looked in horror at the floor. It was sliding open; the air was rushing out. He wanted to grab hold of the rail, the toilet, anything to stop him from being sucked into the white hole. He edged back as far as he could, parallel now to the bowl. It was no good, the gap was coming towards him. Inch by inch it crept forward until the tips of his toes were suspended over the blue sea, 34,000 feet below.

We give our Sea shadow this offering. We send you our sacrifice Mr. Lachlan Driftwood. We give this man thing to the ocean. Accept our gift for free passage across your blue vastness. Take this human offering from your one true family.

He was falling, falling through the white clouds and the freezing cold air. Even though he must be dead Lachlan could see the red flashing lights of the plane disappear into the distance. The ocean was rushing up to meet him, blue water crashing in on top of itself. Millions of faces looking up to meet him, to welcome him into the Sea Shadow. Finally, at home with the fish and the sunken boats. As one with the wreckage of past planes and lost souls. Lachlan was no longer angry, he felt calm, almost happy.

Do you enjoy flying? I mean seriously, do you? No, I thought not. I am glad we finally agree on that. If you do have to fly then can I recommend the scratch cards, oh and the little bottles of wine.

CLOSURE NOTICE

<u>Friday, Dec 15th, 1961</u>

The snow started to fall this morning. Only two days until Briony leaves with the twins. My mood darkens as each hour passes and the thought of them gone. But then I hear the chatter of Alwen and the childish laughter of Tristan from the platform below and it becomes impossible not to smile. I know I should not leave the signal box during my shift but what does it matter now? Only four trains pass each way, three carrying passengers and one goods. The chances of the bell ringing to alert me of any special working have long gone. Two weeks and all this will fall silent, the station, the cottage, everything. Very soon our little home of the last three years will rot and merge into the surrounding countryside as if it never existed.

After the 5:35 pm passed I climbed down from my lofty perch to help Briony with the last of the packing. No trains have called at Llanbadarn Fynyd since 1956 but the Sunday goods train has been organised to stop the day after tomorrow to take my family to our new life in Scotland. How will I survive the next two Weeks without them? I used to kid myself that I loved the solitude of working at this lost and lonely outpost of the Railway, but it was not that. It was the fact that I had Briony and the twins all to myself. Our little self-contained family not even interrupted by the passing trains stopping at our little station.

She put her arms around me as I walked into the cottage. The twins had already started to build a snowman even though there was not yet enough of the white powder to even make a snowball. I wonder if we will get a heavy fall. Maybe it will come down so hard the accountants in London will make the decision to close the line sooner and I too can leave. Wishful thinking, I know, but it is a nice thought none the less.

Saturday, Dec 16th, 1961

I hardly slept last night. I wanted to feel every second of Briony tucked closely beside me. The warmth of her body, the smell of her hair, the sound of gentle breathing. The thought of the twins bursting into our room, full of excitement and anticipation for the coming day. How wonderful it is to see and hear children embrace every second of their childhood. I knew they would see the continuing heavy fall of snow and I would have to help them with the snowman. I was up early at 6 a.m., it still gave me a few hours until the first train of the day passed at 8:13 a.m.

I became so engrossed in laughing with Alwen and Tristan as the snowman rose from the ground that I almost missed the tinkling of the bells from the signal box at the end of the platform. I had to run to pull the levers to let the first train of the day past. Old Arthur was on the footplate and gave his usual wave as they sped past in a hail of snow and hissing steam. Briony climbed the steps of the box soon after with my morning cup of tea. She stayed with me for the next hour as we listened to the children's squeals of delight. No doubt the snowman was getting taller behind the boarded-up station building as the snow continued to fall.

After that, I was left alone for the rest of the day with my lonely thoughts of what the next few weeks would bring once my beloved family left me tomorrow. It was dark and cold when the last train passed. I walked back to the cottage past the opposite end of the station. For some reason, I could not bear to see the snowman. Maybe I had decided never to walk that way again. It would be too painful to look upon that white statue without the children playing beside it.

The fire was burning brightly in the hearth as we all sat around it sharing our last meal together at Llanbadarn Fynyd. As you would expect Briony and the twins could not contain their excitement for the following day's journey to Scotland. I tried to keep a brave face at the thought of them leaving me. Am I a fool to feel like this when I will be reunited with them all in a few short weeks? Why do I feel so lonely already?

Briony could sense how I felt and reminded me that I still had our little cat Puddles to keep me company. He sat on the window ledge looking out at the snow, no doubt wondering how he would catch his next mouse. We had agreed that it would be easier for me to bring him along when I followed them to Scotland in a few weeks.

Sunday, Dec 17th, 1961

They have gone. As arranged, the only train to pass on a

Sunday, the 11:40 a.m. goods stopped at Llanbadarn Fynyd for the first time in five years. The only reason for its existence since the station master locked the doors in 1956 has been the signal box to allow trains to use the passing loop through the station. It was a tearful farewell for all four of us. Has a family ever been so close as me, my beloved Briony and our beautiful twins? I watched as the guard's van at the end of the train disappeared into the snow-covered distance. They waved until I could no longer make out the steam against the snow and all became silent. Oh god, how will I survive two weeks here on my own? I hate this place now; without them, it is a tomb. A sea of white covering me and everything in its deathly silence.

By the afternoon I had cheered up. We would have been leaving Llanbadarn Fynyd next summer even if the railway had not been closing. The twins would have been starting school and with only a dirt road to the village four miles away, it would have been impractical to stay.

With no further trains to signal on a Sunday, I spent the rest of the day in the cottage and drank half of one of my treasured bottles of whisky. I had intended to wait until Christmas day but as usual, my willpower gave out. As I write this in my half inebriation, I suddenly have the urge to go and visit the snowman. It will make me think of the children, of her, it will break the silence that surrounds the little cottage. The snow is falling hard against the door, maybe I will try and clear a path. Anything but sit here alone.

Monday, Dec 18th, 1961

As I reset the levers back to danger following the passing of the 12:37 p.m. I am still smiling at my memories of last night. I am not entirely sure what time it was, but it must have been after midnight. I do remember drunkenly staggering out of the cottage and making a pathetic attempt to clear the track to the station of snow. It was a hopeless task; not only was I drunk but the white powder was drifting hard in the wind. As soon as I swept a path, it quickly filled up again. I do remember abandoning my efforts and heading to the dark forlorn station. It was a mistake not to take a lantern, but the snow seemed to have a luminescence all its own.

And the reason I am still laughing at myself? I must have made a pathetic sight as I tripped over Puddles the cat at the end of the station building where we had built the snowman. He had followed me out into the dark winter and kept running between my legs. All I remember is looking up and feeling startled, then shocked and finally happy. I cannot wait until Briony calls the only phone line in the signal box at 3 o'clock this afternoon. Only then will I be able to thank my wonderful children who, no doubt with the help of their mother worked so hard to leave me some company. Yes, standing at the side of the building was the snowman, at least five feet tall. And beside him? His four-foot snow woman and two little snow children.

Something seems odd. Briony called at 3 p.m. as agreed. It was lovely to hear from her and she even got the twins to shout a quick excited hello down the phone. They are staying with Aunt Clarence in Edinburgh until I join them. Then all of us will go together to our new home in Haddington. As it is a railway telephone, we only had a few minutes to talk. It was only at the end that I remembered the snow people they had made for me. When I mentioned it to Briony, she seemed confused. Maybe Tristan and Alwen made the snow woman and children themselves? But how did they manage to make them so tall? Oh well, it was a lovely gesture no matter how they did it.

Tuesday, December 19th, 1961

My mood is dark today. The snow is starting to cover the railway tracks, but the trains are still running so far. The day is gloomy with little light managing to break through the grey snow-filled sky. Because of this, I have had to keep filling the signal lamps with oil to keep them lit even during daylight hours. It is a miserable task in winter even without the snow. In these conditions, it is even more treacherous as I must climb each ladder to refill the oil and change the wicks. Another thing is worrying me. I have not seen Puddles since I tripped over him on Sunday night. I assume he has climbed into the old station building to hide from the snow.

I was halfway up the signal at the end of the platform when the phone in the signal box rang. I battled through the snow and luckily caught it before the caller rung off. It was Hugh Thomas the station master down at Tylwch. It is the first manned station after Llanbadarn Fynyd, about five miles down the track. Old Hugh and the signalman Rhys Collier are my only daily contact with the outside world. I do occasionally cycle into the village and the grocery van comes once a week, but these two are the only outsiders I need to talk to. You see, I don't need anyone else, just Briony and little Tristan with his dark curls. Close by him you will always find his twin sister Alwen. They are never apart from each other. I suppose in a way, just like the snow children they built for me.

It was a mixture of good and bad news from old Hugh Thomas. British Railways head office had decreed that no more trains would run on my line after the last one this evening, the 7:50 p.m. It seems they had decided it was not worth sending snow ploughs out when the line was due to close on Friday 29th of December. If the snow stopped then they intended to restart but until then I would not even have the company of the signal box bells ringing and the occasional train passing through. I would still have to man the box for safety reasons, but it would be a long day tomorrow and then each day after.

My eyes are not the same, it must be this incessant white powder that still falls. As I pulled the levers back, I could see the 7:50 storm through the little forlorn station. It sprayed snow from the line across the unlit platforms. I was sure I could see a figure standing at the end of the building, the lights from the carriages reflected off it. I knew it must be my imagination, who would be out here at this time. In fact, who the hell could get out here in this drifting white hell. It is only two days since they left. Briony will not be able to phone again until Friday. I felt even more lonely than usual as the red tail lamp of the last train disappeared.

Wednesday, December 20th, 1961

I had a troubled sleep last night. The snow falling on the roof of the cottage was making strange noises. It almost sounded like someone or something was crawling over it above my head. I wondered if it might be Puddles but that was crazy. Why would he climb onto the roof in these conditions? I was too tired to even light the fire yesterday evening. This morning I decided to spend the rest of my time in the signal box. I can keep the fire going in there and sleep on the chair with my blanket. It even has a small outside toilet and a stove for heating the kettle. Anyway, the cottage holds the memories of my family. I miss them more than life itself. I shall spend the rest of the day moving supplies from the cottage to the signal box.

How strange. Even though it still snows hard I could make out the vague prints in the snow before the fresh fall filled them up again. I tried to reason that maybe someone from the village had driven up the road to the station but could see no tyre tracks. I don't understand, there was not just one set of prints but several. Who on earth would be out here? There must be an explanation.

I am laughing for the first time in days. It was the tracks of our cat Puddles of course. The small prints he had made must have become bigger with the impact of the falling snow. That was it, yes that must have been what it was. I will attempt to go out later and try to find him.

It has been another long day. The fire in the signal box is burning brightly and I will admit that the whisky is helping to add to the warm glow. Even though the snow still falls outside, I feel more cheerful now. And the day after tomorrow my love will call and I will hear her and the children's voices once again.

Thursday, December 21st, 1961

My head hurts with the alcohol and the fire is almost out. I woke with a start at 7 a.m. as snow broke away from the roof and tumbled down the side of the box. I feel sick with fear and loneliness but not from the whisky. What in god's name is it? Even through the blinding snow and my poor eyesight I can see it. Something is standing at the far end of the platform, covered in white snow. I am certain it is human but why does it not move, why is it looking at me? I decided to go and investigate but the snow is now so deep it was impossible to leave my lofty perch and climb down the steps to the platform. Maybe the truth was, I did not want to go and see what it was.

I was glad when the darkness came early and along with the falling powder it blocked out everything within a few yards of the signal box. I relit the fire and opened another bottle of whisky. I had hoped to keep some of my prized malts to take to our new home in Scotland but now I needed them more than anything. I could have tried to call Hugh Thomas but what would I have told him? Tomorrow Briony will call from Haddington on the railway telephone. Tomorrow everything will be fine. Maybe even the snow will stop?

Friday, December 22nd, 1961

I have the snow fever, that can be the only explanation. Still, it falls and is now so heavy that I can only see halfway along the platform. At first, that cheered me as I could no longer see the silent figure that watched me from the end of the station building. But, the respite from my torment did not last. By one o'clock in the afternoon, I could see it standing like a statue on the platform. Whatever evil madness was stalking me, it had moved, so now it just appeared at the edge of the snowstorm.

I refused to let it haunt me and re-lit the fire while waiting for my love to make the appointed call at 3 p.m. But the time passed and by 3:30 I could wait no longer. I picked up the phone to call Hugh Thomas at Tylwch station and discovered to my horror that the line was dead. Oh God have mercy on my soul. I am trapped in this coffin-like signal box with the whiteout blocking any exit. And yet, the glass that surrounds the box allows me to see the dim light of the fading day. I shall stay by the fire and not look out. Ignore the creeping madness before it engulfs me.

Please, someone, anyone help me. I drank my fill of whisky and shone the lamp out of the window at midnight. The figure stood still in the swirling snow about ten yards away. Even as I write this, I know it sounds ridiculous. The figure looks like a snowman, it is hard to tell because everything is covered in the evil white powder. And yet, that is not all. As I looked on in horror my eyes could just see them through the swirling snowstorm in the distance. The figure of a white woman and two pale white children. As I write this, I am cowered down on the signal box floor, the fire is almost out. I will drink the rest of the bottle and pray when I wake in the morning that the apparition has gone from my brain.

Saturday, December 23rd, 1961

My prayers have been answered. The snow has stopped, although the sky tells me that more will come before the end of the day. Of course, the apparitions in my mind have gone. From this day on I will never touch a drop of the hard stuff again. Alcohol and the snow have driven me to the edge of sanity for the last time. I have made my decision; I will abandon the signal box and fight my way back to the cottage. If the snow stays off, I shall attempt to get through to the village or at least the nearest farm with a phone line. I hate the thought of leaving my post but surely there can be no way that the trains will run until the snow and communication problems are solved.

I am still shaking with fear and shock. From the lofty signal box, the snow looked bad, but nothing could have prepared me for the battle ahead. It took me three hours using the shovel and my bare hands to finally make the few hundred yards to the cottage. What insanity possessed me to think that I could make it to the village? To make matters worse, when I finally dug my way to the cottage door, I found the body of Puddles. He lay frozen solid as though he had been trying desperately to get back into the building. Why did I leave the poor animal to fend for itself? At least the cottage has enough wood and food to see me through the next few days until help arrives. To make matters worse, it has started snowing again. I dare not attempt to go out again, even to get back to my post.

The madness came back just after midnight. I had convinced myself not to drink but still, it returned. As I sat in my chair in front of the fire with only the wind and drifting snow to keep me company, I heard a familiar sound. It was surely impossible; no trains could run through this. But, the tinkling of the bell was telling me that a train was being sent into my section. I peered out of the window and strained to hear the sound, praying it would stop. The signal box bell still rang but that no longer mattered. It was back, they were back. The snow family had reached within a few yards of the cottage door and they all stared directly at me.

Sunday, December 24th, 1961

I woke at midday on Sunday, my head pounding. I must have looked a pathetic sight, my eyes black with drinking and fear. Last night I drew all the curtains and retreated into the cellar with the last few bottles. I no longer care; I will remain here until rescue comes. The snow still falls and until it stops the madness will continue. I intend to remain hidden in this tiny dark room, safe from both real life and my imagination.

The soft knocking on the cottage door started a few hours ago. No matter how much I drink it will not block out the incessant tapping. I know it is them, the snow family. Whether they are real or imagined does not matter. I realise now that they have come for me and that I will never see Briony or my children again. I dream of my family as the appointed time draws ever nearer. Yes, this is it, I hear the door opening. They will slowly creep over to the cellar. It might take an hour or so, but they will come. I will drink this last bottle in one go and hope that when they open the cellar door, I will be too far gone to look at them face to face.

Extract from the book, Ghost Stations of Wales.
(Published in 2010)

Chapter 5: Snowstorm at Llanbadarn Fynyd

There is a certain melancholy and sadness that goes along with writing a book about closed railway lines. Not only the fact that so much Victorian engineering and human effort went into their building, but also the lives of the many generations they touched. Nothing could have prepared me for the sad tale of Llanbadarn Fynyd station on the lonely line that linked Newtown with Llandrindod Wells in the shadow of the Cambrian Mountains. This is not only a tale of a long-lost railway line but also a tragic human story.

The Newtown to Llandrindod Wells line was scheduled to close on and from Friday 29th December 1961. Most of the stations along the line had already closed to passengers in 1956 but four trains each way continued to run for the next few years to serve a handful of larger settlements such as Tylwch. The station at Llanbadarn Fynyd was one of those to close early but it was still manned by a signalman who looked after the lonely signal box there. The post was not a popular one amongst local railwaymen as the station was extremely remote and lay at least four miles from its namesake village.

According to press reports at the time, the snow started to fall on Friday 15th December 1961. Anyone who lived through that winter in Britain will recall the incredible hardship that most had to suffer. This proved to be even worse in remote areas and Llanbadarn Fynyd was hit extremely hard. Within four days of the first snowflakes, the trains on the line had been cancelled. The downfall continued for almost two weeks and at some points reached the top of the telephone poles. The roads proved to be impassable and the first rescue team to reach Llanbadarn Fynyd was the railway snow plough which finally broke through on the bright afternoon of Friday 29th December. Ironically this was also the day that the line had been scheduled to close for good. I will let the Tylwch station master Hugh Thomas take up the story as reported in the press at the time.

It was my job, in fact, it would prove to be my last job on the Newtown Llandrindod Wells line, to organise the snow ploughs and try to clear the tracks. It seemed odd to me that British Railways would spend so much time and effort to re-open a line that they were just about to close. I was glad they did though as a few of the signalmen at the most remote stations had been stranded for almost two weeks in the blizzard. One of these was young Jim Dunbar who had taken on the Llanbadarn Fynyd job a few years earlier. He seemed a nice young man, but I know he had moved to Wales from Scotland after a troubled past. Even though the phone wires had been brought down by the snow I was not overly worried about Jim or the other stranded men. I knew they would have had plenty of wood and food supplies to get by for at least a few weeks.

We used three steam locomotives coupled together with the plough on the front one. Even with this amount of power it still proved difficult to drive through the snow. We had over thirty men in the wagons behind us to shovel the rest of the snow from the line as we blasted it to the sides. It was around 2 p.m. before we finally got through to Llanbadarn Fynyd. By then the snow had stopped and the first thaw had set in. The old station was a real site as the white powder had drifted almost to the roof of the building. I remember thinking something was not right as; unlike the other blocked stations no attempt had been made to clear any paths through the snow.

We finally cleared a track to Jim's cottage after an hour or so and had to break in as there was no answer at the door. I assumed he had left and tried to get to the village as there was no sign of him. I will always regret not making a more thorough search of the building but at the time we had no cause for alarm. It was another week before the local policeman discovered his body. Once the snow had cleared enough for the roads to become passable and still no sign of Jim, we reported him as missing.

P.C Edwards was a good friend of mine and I will never forget him calling at Tylwch to say he had found the body of Jim Dunbar. For some reason, he was discovered in the cellar and had frozen to death. It was no surprise to me to hear that he was surrounded by empty whisky bottles. I knew Jim liked his whisky but during his time working at Llanbadarn Fynyd I had never known him to be drunk on duty. I suppose I turned a bit of a blind eye to it as I knew the circumstances that had driven him to leave his railway job at Haddington station in Scotland. How sad that he should die in such tragic circumstances only a few years after he lost his wife Briony when she passed away during childbirth. I know he missed her so much as well as the unborn child. There was even a rumour that she might have been expecting twins when she died. God rest his soul and god rest Llanbadarn Fynyd. Both gone now.

Postscript

If you drive along the A602 and take the turning for Tylwch
onto the B4589 then keep going for just over two miles,
you might see it. A slight rise in the road even though the
surrounding fields are flat. Pull into the side of the road
and walk back to the little incline. You will notice two old
walls on either side directly opposite each other. If you take
a closer look it will soon become apparent that these are not
walls at all but the parapets of a long filled in overbridge. At
one time this was the point where the B4589 crossed the
long-closed Newtown Llandindrod Wells railway. Not only
that but just beside the left-hand parapet, you might see an
overgrown track heading down into a small wood. That my
dear friend is the old railway to Llanbadarn Fynyd station.
The little clump of trees has grown over the remains of the
building. Unfortunately, there is nothing to see anymore as
nature has reclaimed the railway line back into the landscape.

The two walls and the faintest of scars in the fields are
all that you can see now to remind you of passing steam
trains, lonely stations and the men who worked the levers
in the signal boxes. Have a thought for a lost time and then
jump back in the car and drive to the village of Llanbadarn
Fynyd for a pint at the Flying Fox on the main street. Oh,
and just one thing. Pray that the sky does not darken, and
the first flakes of snow start to settle around you.

WINTER
(THE TALL MAN)

Is it just a coincidence that the seasons of the year perfectly reflect the cycle of human life? Spring is the season of birth as new growth sprouts from the earth. Summer is the flourishing as colour and youth spread across the ground. Then the wise season of Autumn arrives, life is still a clash of beautiful violent shades despite being on the wane. But soon the glory of the falling leaves becomes shaded by the bare branches as winter arrives. Death sits on our doorstep and surrounds us in the bleak dark cold.

You might find this hard to imagine but despite most of my books being about ghosts, I don't particularly believe there is such a thing. Now don't get me wrong, I agree there is so much that we frail little human beings do not understand. Why do we exist? What is our purpose? Is there a God? And so on. I accept we know so little that maybe ghosts and a million other things we don't understand could indeed be on our doorstep. Probably like most other cynical males of my mature years, I tend to believe only what I see. Well, that was how I thought until yesterday and then things changed.

Now, I know what you are thinking. This guy writes ghost stories, so he is good at telling tall tales, but I promise, what I am about to tell you is true. It has got me wondering if something my wife mentioned in the past has come back to haunt me. She believes that if you attract negative energy then it will eventually search you out. Does that mean if you write ghost stories then you are destined to see ghosts?

I try to cycle once a week along an old road that has been turned into a bike track. This road runs parallel to the new motorway although at times it meanders far enough away that you can no longer hear any traffic. As winter edges nearer my weekly outings become more sporadic until they eventually peter out with the dark nights and freezing rain. The run is about ten miles and then the old road re-joins the motorway and I turn back. In the summer it is a pleasant journey past damp moorland and dark fir trees. The occasional field and distant farm can be seen but other than that it can be a lonely journey. A few cars may pass and sometimes another cyclist will nod or smile hello to you as they hurtle along in lycra and wraparound sunglasses. I do this run to keep fit but I do it at a pace that suits my mature years. Think of me as Winter now but maybe just having left Autumn.

It was yesterday, November 26th that I went on the bike run I am going to tell you about. It was the first time I had managed to get out for weeks due to the incessant wet Scottish climate. I checked the weather app a few days before and it told me it would be dry although the temperature would only climb to 6 degrees. I set out at 7 am in the morning, three layers of clothing covering me. No lycra as I am too old for that, but I will admit to the wrap-around shades. By 7.30 I had left the edges of Glasgow and hit the track. It was bitterly cold and to make matters worse a freezing damp mist clung to the ground making visibility extremely poor. If all this sounds like a poor imitation of the setting for Dracula, I swear on my life, it was exactly as I describe it.

It usually takes me about an hour to reach the turnaround point but because it was so cold and misty, I lacked motivation. Cycling is like most forms of exercise; you have to push yourself to do it but once you start, the adrenalin kicks in and it becomes exhilarating. But not yesterday. From the minute I left my house I kept questioning why I was out in this cold. I suppose I expected the mist to lift and the low winter sun to come out, but it never did. I battled on to the halfway point and with a feeling of relief, I started heading back. A few miles into my return journey I always stop at the same point to take a drink from my water bottle. I do it because it feels right to take time out and admire the scenery. That little feeling of achievement, a small celebration to acknowledge I have almost completed another run. There was no scenery to admire this time around, just wet clinging mist that swirled around everything.

At this point, the old road edges onto a small forest of conifer trees. The other side skirts an old quarry built into a hill. It too is covered with trees but not as dense as the side I am on. I always rest my bike on an old wooden gate before taking out my water bottle and having the obligatory look at my phone. I always wondered why the gate was there and on a previous summer visit I clambered over it and followed an old path. It eventually petered out some distance away at the edge of the motorway. I assume that before the new road was built it once led to a house or a farm. I remember that sunny day well because on the way back I again attempted to climb the old gate and part of it collapsed underneath me. Time and Scottish weather are not kind to mankind's abandoned efforts.

I know it sounds like a cliché but maybe that is why things that happen so often do sound like a cliché. As I looked at my phone, I could tell someone, or something was watching me. At this point I did not have any fear, I just automatically turned to face the other side of the gate. The visibility was still only ten yards or so, but I could see him quite clearly. Staring at me from the trees was an old man. He stood perfectly still, shrouded by the conifers and the mist. His hair was as grey as his face and he wore a long coat that almost came down to his feet. It was difficult to make out how old he was, but I reckon he must have been in his eighties. Now, this is the point where the ice gripped my heart. It was not his age or even the knowledge that he had come from the mist to stare at me, it was this. He was tall, way too tall to be normal. Maybe the whole situation got to me, but I swear he might have been seven feet or more. He was long and thin, and he just stood there.

I must have a bit of that British stiff upper lip in me or could it be I hate the thought of embarrassing myself. I should have fled but instead, I simply ignored him while quickly replacing my water bottle onto the bike. I picked the cycle up and methodically climbed onboard. Maybe I was thinking that if I did not panic then like a cornered animal he would not attack. I had to look, but only once I had made the first revolution of the pedals and moved that first few feet. I had to know that I was going to escape before reacquainting myself with the tall staring man. I swear to God and I still have a cold sweat when I think about it. He was moving. Maybe it was the long coat and I could not see his legs, but he was gliding. Floating out of the mist towards the gate and in my fucking direction. At that point I became an Olympic cyclist, I was gone, and I did not look back until I saw the first houses of civilisation appear through the mist.

I drove back there this morning; I even talked my wife into coming with me. The sun was out and although it is a naturally eerie spot, everything looked normal. I walked to the gate and like some kind of tracker I searched for footprints. Of course, I found nothing but what does that prove? All I will say is, I know what I saw. I have tried to rationalise it; it could have been anyone. What is so unusual about a person standing at the edge of a forest? Yes, I agree that is true. But, why would an old man be there on a freezing misty early morning? In the middle of nowhere, with no means of transport. I did not see any cars parked;

they would have stuck out as there is nowhere to stop. Why did he not speak? I will tell you why, because he was the walking dead. I don't care what anyone else tells me, I am a logical person. I know what I saw, and it has me wondering if I should continue to write ghost stories. I don't know. That's winter for you.

DUST IN THE WIND

(In the land of Cinnamon Bob)

'Are you being fucking serious?' Finn eyed up Paul across the table. He knew that after five pints of Scotland's national drink the conversation would drift into plans that would never happen in the cold light of a sober morning.

'Yes, I fucking am. Trust me on this one Finn, if we get the tickets, then why not. What better way could we possibly find to give Big Tony the perfect send-off.' Finn nodded his head in agreement. This would all be forgotten about tomorrow and even if Paul was serious, two obstacles stood in their way. Firstly, the hope of them getting tickets for the upcoming Scotland v England game at Wembley would be zero. Even more unlikely, the chance of convincing Big Tony's wife to let them borrow his ashes for the trip would be a lot less than zero.

'But what about Big Isobel. She would frighten the shite out of a ghost. No way is she going to let us take a dead Tony to London with us. Fuck, even if he was still alive, she would not have let him go on the trip. She only hates one person more than me, and that is you.' The two young men fell into a few minutes of silence as they remembered their departed friend, Big Tony. He had exited this mortal world only twelve months before. The tree he had wrapped his motorbike around on the A74 near Elvanfoot still bore the scratch marks. Unfortunately for Big T, he incurred a few more serious injuries than the large Pine had suffered. Let's just say, they needed more than one ambulance to transport his scattered remains to the local morgue.

'You just leave Big Isobel to me. Unlike you, I am not scared of that fat cow. You just let your Uncle Paul sort her out.' Finn burst out laughing. Both men knew that this was just the drink talking. Tony's wife would eat Paul for breakfast, she would eat all three of them for breakfast.

'Anyway, none of this matters. Jake is full of shite. He has no chance of getting tickets. He probably did not even send the letter to get us into the ballot.' Paul nodded in agreement although he was still thinking about how he could tackle Big Isobel.

The door of The Macdonald Arms burst open and Jake hurried in. His face was red with exertion, it would soon be even more crimson with the effect of multiple pints of lager. He shouted over a quick hello to his two friends before storming up to the bar. The burley barman, Cinnamon Bob eyed him up. 'Well if it isn't the final part of the Coatbridge Tartan army. What can I get you Mr. Finn the Bruce, a sherry, a little glass of white wine…' Jake quickly cut the publican off before he could continue his tirade.

'A pint of McEwan's you cheeky big bastard. And, anyway, it is rude to mock the dead. Poor Tony is only in his grave twelve months and you are taking the piss out of him.' Cinnamon Bob laughed causing his large head to shake and the multitude of long curls to flutter around his face.

'Listen you, scruffy little kilted warrior. I would have said the same to Big Tony when he was alive. I would say the same to all four of you, little runts, so stop fucking moaning.' He pushed the glass of flat lager towards Jake, some of it spilling out of the tumbler and onto the bar. Jake picked it up and took a long gulp of the cold liquid before placing it back down. He turned to face Paul and Finn who sat deep in conversation at one of the tables.

'Guys. I have something to announce, something that

will shut up this big ugly bastard at the bar once and for all.' He reached slowly and dramatically into his coat to pull something out of the top pocket. Cinnamon Bob used the few seconds of silence to get another dig in.

'Don't tell me you are going to get a sex change. I always thought you three guys were little girls anyway.' Jake ignored the barman and continued his performance. By now all the scattered occupants of the pub were looking at him, waiting to hear what the announcement would be. He pulled out some little bits of paper and waved them in the air.

'In my hand boys, I have three, yes three pieces of card. Do you want to know what is written on each of the three gorgeous, lovely, kissable bits of pure gold I now hold in my hand?' Even Cinnamon Bob had shut up as the anticipation levels rose for everyone listening.

'Well let me fucking tell you then. On this little card it says, Admit one to Wembley Stadium for England V Scotland on June 4th, 1977.' He placed the object back in his coat and then went through the same performance for all three tickets. Even the belligerent barman stood open-mouthed. Tickets for the bi-annual auld enemy clash were like gold dust. The fact that Jake had managed to get hold of three was no mean feat. He turned with a look of joy on his face, matched only by both Paul and Finn before shouting at the top of his lungs and pointing at his friends.

'Boys we are leaving this little shithole called Coatbridge on the evening of June 3rd and we, yes fucking we, are going to WEMBERLEEEEEEE.'

He ran over to the table and all three of the young men jumped around in a circle while holding each other. Cinnamon Bob shook his head and continued to wipe the spilt beer from the bar before throwing in his final comment.

'You three are that fucking stupid you will probably end up as rent boys. London is a big place and you dumb school kids have never been further than the fucking High Street in Coatbridge.'

Suddenly Paul stopped jumping up and down and grabbed Jake. All three stood looking at each other wondering what was wrong. Paul looked to be deep in thought before he finally spoke.

'Fuck, we forgot something.' Jake answered him with a worried frown.

'What, what did we forget?'

'We need four tickets, not three. Four tickets for fuck sake Jake, Four tickets.' Jake gave him a half-serious puzzled look.

'Why Paul, there are only three of us.'

'We need another ticket. Big Tony is coming with us too. Well, his fucking ashes are.' The three of them started laughing and jumping around again while holding each other up. It was Finn who spoke last, but through the shouting, no one could hear him.

'Well Paul, all you need to do now is sort out Big Isobel and get hold of Tony's ashes.

(Big Isobel becomes unreasonable)

The three boys sat at their usual table in the McDonald Arms looking very glum. At least it was Cinnamon Bob's night off, so they would not have to listen to his endless mocking. Tomorrow would be June 3rd and they would be getting one of the overnight football specials from Glasgow Central railway station. They along with thousands of other marauding Scottish drunks would arrive in London on the morning of the big match. Everything was sorted out, even the much older Cinnamon Bob had relented from continually deriding them. He was going to take his battered Cortina and drive them to Glasgow to get the train down South. The boys had earned the respect from the locals, they had tickets, home-made kilts, flags, scarfs and 36 cans of Tennant's lager for the trip. What could possibly go wrong?

'So, tell me again. What did she say when you asked her?' Finn had heard what his tall friend Paul had said, he was just enjoying the moment. Paul knew this but repeated the story anyway while he tried to think of a way around the problem.

'The fat cow slammed the door in my face but not before screaming, My Tony would not be fucking dead if he had been sensible and not hung around with you bunch of fucking losers. Are you bloody serious, I mean his ashes, his fucking ashes? You are going where, London, fucking London, what the fuck.' Paul shook his head as Jake offered his tuppence worth.

'Was she angry?' the two other boys looked at him with incredulity.

'What! No, she was smiling and laughing. What the fuck do you think she was Jake? Of course, she was fucking angry, at one point she even started fucking crying.'

The three boys shook their heads at the thought of Big Isobel being so unreasonable. For a few minutes, they sat in silence. Finn knew this was a bad sign. When Paul became quiet, it usually meant he was thinking up another plan. One that would involve him and usually end up in trouble. Paul picked up his pint glass and took a long drink before speaking.

'Well, there is only one thing we can do then.' The other two boys watched him in anticipation.

'We shall have some more beers, lots more in fact. And then, when we leave here we shall go up to big Isobel's and break-in. Simple, we steal Big T's ashes, it will be easy.' Jake laughed and nodded in agreement, while Finn stared at him with a look of disbelief spread across his face.

(Big Tony does a runner)

The three eighteen-year-old boys stood with their backs to the wall of the house. It was pitch black, but the scruffy overgrown garden could have kept them concealed on its own. Only one light shone from the house and Paul had decided that it must be from the bedroom. Despite it being nearly midnight, they could hear the sound of Leo Sayer crooning, *when I need you*, floating out of the slightly open bedroom window. They agreed this might not be the best point of entry. None of the three fancied landing on the bed beside Big Isobel. A quick scout around the rest of the house had incredibly found the back door unlocked. A drunken talk ensued as they argued who should go inside and free Big Tony. They all knew it was a pointless exercise, but they went through the discussion anyway. Finn was far too sensible and a coward, Jake was too bloody stupid and would get them caught. It had to be their leader Paul. He was the tallest, the craziest and anyway, it had all been his idea.

Paul tried his best to be quiet as he edged through the dark hallway. It was difficult to be a house breaker after six pints, his body tended to want to go in a different direction to what his brain was telling him. He could see light creeping out from the underneath of the bedroom door. The music had now switched to Abba belting out their latest smash, Dancing Queen. *Big Tony's ashes had to be in the living room.* Paul was praying they would not be in the bedroom with the mountain of a woman he had married. She had been more than ten years older than him, a strange couple. Most felt she had been punching above her weight, difficult when you consider she must be at least twenty stone. They only called him Big Tony to be ironic. In reality, he had been barely five foot two. An eighteen-year-old with a woman of thirty who looked as though she had eaten him. yes, a strange couple indeed.

Paul tried to concentrate; his mind was wandering through the influence of the alcohol. For some reason, he felt himself edging towards the bedroom door. It was only when he became level with it that he realised it was slightly open. He crept forward and placed his eye up to the gap to look through. The sight that greeted him was not what he expected. Inside he could make out Big Isobel's naked backside bouncing up and down on the bed. He looked in utter disbelief as the two bodies merged in a sea of blubber and clashing flesh. Suddenly he stumbled forward and fell through the door, finally finding his feet just before he nearly tumbled onto the bed. Big Isobel slid off her victim to allow Cinnamon Bob to regain his breath and stare at Paul in shock.

Finn and Jake had already taken to their heels. They were laughing hysterically as they plunged towards the gate at the end of the overgrown garden. Behind them came the figure of Paul running like a banshee. Further behind them framed by the now floodlit house came the naked mass of bouncing jelly known as Big Isobel. The boys were too fast for her as she screamed at the trio disappearing into the black night. 'Ya fucking wee bastards, I know who you are. You are fucking dead when I get hold of you.' She had a large object in her hand and in one last desperate act of revenge she hurled it up into the air. It came crashing down on the road beside Paul and rolled down the hill along with the three escapees. Back at the house, the nude figure of Cinnamon Bob stood chuckling as he watched the commotion in front of him.

The three young men finally stopped running when they realised that Big Isobel had given up the chase. Finn was desperately trying to catch his breath from both the exertion and laughing as he bent down to pick up the object the woman had flung at them. 'What did the big cow throw at us?' Finn looked back at Paul, a large grin spread across his face.

'It looks like Big Tony is going to make the trip to Wembley after all.' Paul winked at Jake before walking over to take the urn of ashes from Finn.

'Did I not tell you guys to leave me to sort out Big Isobel?'

(The Flying Scotsman)

It was nearing midnight at what would normally have been a very quiet Glasgow Central. The last trains would usually have been pulling out, a few drunk stragglers making a late dash to grab the ride home. Tonight, it was different, very different. Four long disorderly queues snaked around the concourse. Each one a sea of tartan and cheap kilts. Young males, most of them inebriated, sang and chanted at the top of their lungs. Nearly all still wore their hair long. The burgeoning punk culture had yet to fully invade Scotland even this late in 1977. Despite the excited noise and revelry, the mood was good. Even the normally dour Glaswegian Police had taken an evening off from handing out instant justice. They marched up and down trying to keep some semblance of order although it was proving to be a thankless task. Four football specials would be leaving just after midnight. British Rail had assembled these trains from every rusty scrap siding they could find across Scotland. The trains would be a mess by the time they arrived in London so it hardly mattered.

All three boys wore home-made kilts. Paul and Finn both had their blue Scotland tops on while Jake had decided to go topless although he wore so many tartan scarfs it would have been difficult to notice. He had at least three wrapped around his head, four around his waist and one on each wrist. Suddenly one of the lines of young men broke out into a chorus of, *if you hate the fucking English, clap your hands, if you hate the fucking English clap your hands.* Soon thousands of voices had joined in the chant followed by a mass of drunken clapping. The Police ignored the racket and continued to push the throng towards the waiting carriages.

The train was making steady progress through the night and at 2 am it seemed to be slowing up for a stop. Finn and Paul had managed to grab a seat, Big Tony's remains placed tightly between them. Many were left to stand including Jake. No one cared, the cans of lager were flowing, and the toilets were already blocked. Most were now simply taking a pee in the corners or anywhere they could find. Finn strained his eyes to look through the dirty window of the carriage. 'Why are we stopping, where the fuck are, we?' It was Jake who answered, shouting at the top of his voice.

'It's fucking London. We are in fucking London guys; can you believe it.' Paul took a swig from his can of lager and laughed.

'Don't be such a dick, Jake. It's a bloody train, not a

fucking rocket. Carlisle, it says Carlisle. It's another six hours to London you fucking eejit. We are only just across the border into England.'

The train juddered to a halt just outside the impressive cavern of Carlisle station. No doubt the procession of football specials going south would be slowing things up. The carriages had stopped beside a massive retaining wall that dropped around fifty feet down to a taxi rank below. One of the late-night cab drivers had got out of his car as he heard the strains of *dirty English bastards, dirty English bastards,* being belted out from the kilted choir. He then made the big mistake of deciding to stand up for his nation. The rotund taxi driver started to gesticulate at the train above him. Within seconds a sea of both empty and full lager cans was bouncing off the bodywork of his shiny black cab. He was only saved by the sudden movement of the train as the glimmering red railway signal turned to a bright green.

'Paul, I am bursting to do a pee.' Finn looked like a worried man as he whispered the words to his tall friend seated beside him.

'Well just take a leak in the carriage, everyone else is.' Finn still looked concerned despite the rather obvious advice from his mate.

'I can't fucking pee when there are loads of people around watching me.' Paul turned and looked at Finn.

'Well it is either that or you pee your fucking pants. If you decide on the latter, then let me know. I am not sitting next to you smelling of pish.' Paul took a final drink from his can of lager before throwing it under the table. He bent down to retrieve another one from the plastic bag at his feet and slowly placed his finger around the ring pull before sliding it open.

'Do you want one Finn? By the time you have another few of these beauties you will be so desperate, you won't care who watches you doing a piss.' Finn leaned back in his seat to get comfortable.

'No fucking thanks, Paul. As always, you have been a great help. I shall sit it out, surely this heap of a train will stop at a station somewhere and I can nip out to the toilet.' Paul laughed before offering further advice.

'You should have taken the opportunity back at Carlisle and done it on that fat English taxi driver.'

(Finn takes a toilet break)

It was nearing four o'clock in the morning and most of the train had quietened down. Some had fallen asleep either in their seats or on any free space they could find on the floor. There still remained a hardcore who intended to party until they arrived in London at 7 am. This included Jake who was leading a conga up and down the carriage to a chorus of *Jimmy Hills a poof*. The famous English football pundit had long been a target for the Tartan hoards and tonight he was getting the full treatment. Paul was nodding off, his head bobbing up and down as he half drifted into sleep. Just when it looked like he had finally hit the land of slumber, his arm would move the can of lager to his lips for another swig. Finn sat beside him, his eyes wide open and a worried frown across his face. *Surely this fucking train will stop soon. If not, I am going to have to pee myself.*

It soon became too much for Finn and he climbed over Paul to go and find the toilet. 'Where the fuck are you going?'

'I need to find a bog. I can't wait any longer. Keep my seat for me. Don't let any of these arseholes grab it while I am away.' Paul ignored him and stretched back to make himself more comfortable.

Finn edged his way carefully over the piles of discarded lager cans and prone bodies on the floor of the train. The conga line led by Jake came hurtling towards him, still singing but by now they had changed the words to a home-made version. *He's a poof, he's a poof oh yes, a fucking poof.* No doubt many on the train could associate themselves with the sentiment of the song, but this was the seventies. You kept it quiet, even more so on a testosterone-filled carriage full of Scottish warriors about to invade England. He finally found the toilet and tried to open the door. It would not budge. Finn put his arm against it and pushed. 'The fuck are ye up to ya fucking bam.' At least three bodies had jammed into the little room to sleep. One of them was a very large Dundonian who did not take kindly to an intruder invading his makeshift bedroom.

Finn beat a hasty retreat. He could feel the pressure as if his bladder was about to burst. There was only one thing left to do. He looked up at the little sign that said, *Emergency communication chord. Misuse will be liable to a fine of up to £50.* His hand reached to grab the little silver chain and he pulled it down. Within seconds the train started to break and shudder. It finally ground to a halt in the black night.

Finn pulled open the nearest door expecting to have to drop three or four feet to the ground. Incredibly the train had stopped at a station and he found himself standing on a dark platform. He knew he would have to act with haste before he was blamed for the stop and ran quickly into the shadows of the little station building. Just a few yards away Paul was peering through the window laughing at the figure of his friend disappearing into the night.

The guard was already running along the platform to the front of the train shouting to be heard over the strains of, *He's a poof, oh he's a poof, a great big poof.* The driver poked his head out the window. He could vaguely make out the words of his colleague. 'Get the fucking train moving, it's just one of those eejits who pulled the chord, ignore it.' Within seconds the driver was pulling the lever to get the massive diesel engine going again.

Paul watched in horror as the train started moving, he could make out the shape of Finn taking a leak in the shadows. He ran to the open door and shouted, 'Get fucking back on Finn you eejit. You are going to be left behind.' By now the head of the conga had arrived beside him with a red-faced Jake in front.

'What the fuck's going on Paul?'

'It's Finn, he is going to be left behind.'

The object of their panic could not move. The waterfall that had lain constrained inside him for so long would not stop. Finn could hear the train roaring away behind him but the relief from unloading endless pints of liquid was all he could think about.

Paul could see the end of the platform rushing towards him, it was either now or never. He ran back to his seat and grabbed Big Tony's urn before heading back to the door. Just as he was about to jump, he turned to Jake. 'Wait for us outside Wembley. Don't lose the fucking tickets you dozy bastard.' And then he jumped, out into the dark night. The train had already gone past the end of the platform and Paul was sailing through the air along with Big Tony. Back on the train, Jake had already re-started the drunken conga. *Oh, Jimmy Hills a poof, oh Jimmy Hills a poof.*

(Hamford-Slapton's last train)

Finn stood on the dark empty platform with a look of disbelief written across his face. He could see the red taillight of the last carriage disappearing towards London as the cold lonely night surrounded him. The contrast between the drunken chanting mob and the solitude of the lonely station could not have been more pronounced. It was only then that he noticed the shadow creeping along the end of the platform towards him. 'Finn, you fucking tool. Why could you not just pee in the carriage the same as everyone else? Why do you always have to be so bloody different?'

The two boys searched around the little station building but it is was locked up. Paul lit up a cigarette and sat down on the only bench they could find on the platform. 'What are we going to do Paul?' His tall friend took a long drag on the cigarette before calmly replying.

'Not a problem. We simply sit here and wait for the next train.' Finn could only make out the yellow glow of Paul's cigarette. His friend was not thinking straight, but then he had consumed a lot more beer than Finn.

'Paul, I hate to be the one with the bad news, but I think we need to take a few things into account.'

'And what would that be Finn? You are such a worrier. Next train comes, we get on it, catch up with Jake in London and fuck the English at football. What else could we possibly need to consider?' Finn waited a few seconds as he added up the potential problems they might face.

'Ok, Paul. Well, let me fucking think about this one.

First of all, it is four in the morning and we have no idea where this station is. Next, football specials don't fucking call here unless some eejit needs a pee and pulls the emergency stop. Secondly, that means we will need to get a service train and who knows when the first one will be. Thirdly, how much fucking money do you have because I have only got six quid. And last but not least, we left the fucking beer on the train.' Paul stood up and threw his cigarette end on the ground. He pulled up his kilt to check inside his underpants to find the money he had hidden from potential thieves.

'Yes, now you come to mention it, you do have a fair point. I have two quid. And before you start fucking moaning can I point something out. We had our train tickets, beer and football tickets. We would not have needed money if you had pissed on the train instead of acting like a big fucking Jessie.'

Despite it being June, the cool night air was beginning to bite. Neither boy had anything to wear other than their thin kilts and football tops. They picked up Big Tony's urn and decided to explore the little station building to try and ascertain when the first train would be in the morning. Paul reckoned they were near Northampton and only a few hours from London. They could still easily make it in time to meet Jake before the three o'clock kick-off. They walked around to the front of the station. Even in the poor light, they could see the car park was empty and that the little building was surrounded by countryside. Despite using his lighter to guide them Finn tripped over some discarded metal buckets laying at the front of the building. 'Fuck sake, the English must be clatty bastards, this station is a fucking shambles.'

He lifted his lighter to read a poster that was pinned to the locked main door. Paul edged up behind him. 'What does it say, Finn, when is the first train in the morning?' His friend did not answer as he read the words in front of the flickering naked flame. Finally, he turned to face Paul.

'It says, Hamford-Slapton train station will close as and from June 12th, 1968. Your nearest train station is Northampton 24 miles away. We are fucked Paul, fucked. We missed the last train to Wembley nine fucking years ago.' Paul lifted Big Tony's urn to his face and spoke to it.

'Just ignore this negative bastard Big T. We are going to Wembley; this is just another small problem that needs to be negotiated.'

(Jimmy Hill's a poof)

Dawn was breaking over the green countryside. The cold night air was fading away to be replaced by the first rays of the early morning sun. The two young men had stood for a few seconds looking at the sign with dismay. In one direction it read, Cross-Funtley 5 miles, and in the other direction, Hamford-Slapton 4 miles. Without talking they headed off towards the village that had given the railway station its name. The winding road was encompassed by tall hedges on either side. Every few yards a gap would give them a glimpse of rolling fields and lush flowering trees. Finn stopped for a few seconds and breathed in the clear air. 'You know something, Paul?'

'What, what is it now. Will you get a fucking move on, we need to find Slutty-Trumpton or whatever it is fucking called? Grab a taxi and get to Northampton. I hope to God that idiot Jake does not lose our tickets.'

'Don't you think it is really nice here? I mean smell the country air; everything is so green.' Paul turned and glared at him.

'Nice? It is fucking England, you traitor. We are here to fuck them at football, not admire their fucking countryside.

Jeez Finn, sometimes I wonder if you are really Scottish. Next, you will be telling me you have fallen in love with Bobby Charlton.' The two boys laughed as Paul resumed walking. His fast pace meant Finn had to break into a run to catch up.

They walked side by side, both boys lost in their thoughts until once again Finn stopped. This time Paul did the same and faced his friend without speaking.

'I have been thinking about things, Paul. Maybe it's this trip, the whole thing but it has me wondering.'

'Wondering about what Finn?'

'It's just that…well. I am asking myself what the hell we are doing here. I mean it's ok for you, you have a job back in Coatbridge, decent parents. You always seem to have women swooning over you. What have I got to go back to in that one-horse town? An alcoholic dick of a father and fuck all chance of getting a decent job.' Paul placed his hand on his friend's shoulder.

'It's you who is the lucky one Finn, at least you are normal. Things will work out; you are a smart guy.' For a few seconds, they said nothing until Finn broke the silence.

'What do you mean Paul? The bit about me being normal.' He asked the question, but he already knew the answer. He had always known but the two friends kept the pact and it was never mentioned. Finn had watched as the local girls in Coatbridge queued up to flirt with the tall handsome Paul and yet it never led to anything. He always had girl friends but never a girlfriend. Paul did not answer but his eyes seemed to water as he turned without speaking and carried on walking.

They could hear the sound of the approaching car from miles away. It was the first human noise they had heard since the train had unceremoniously left them behind. 'Right Finn, leave this to your Uncle Paul.' The motor suddenly appeared around a bend in the road. It looked like an old Bentley, something from the 1950s. Paul jumped out in front of it waving his arms. The car stopped and an old lady popped her head out of the window.

'Oh, my dear girls, what on earth are you doing out alone at this time of the morning?' Paul gave a confused look at Finn before it suddenly dawned on him that she had probably never seen a man in a kilt before.

'Good morning madam. We are trying to get to Slutty-Trumpton. Unfortunately, our train broke down on the way to the big game. It would be awfully fortunate if you could give us a ride to the village.' Finn shook his head in disbelief, he expected the old woman to drive off to the nearest Police station. Paul was even talking like some sort of English Lord. He did not need to worry. Within seconds Paul had another woman eating out of his hand and both of them jumped into the back of the car.

'I must apologise. I really did think you were two girls with those skirts on. My name is Lady Jane Fetherington but please call me Jane. Are you going to a fancy dress?' Paul ignored her and lit up a cigarette, leaving Finn to do the explaining.

'No, we are on our way to the game. Scotland is playing England in London, Mrs. Fetherington.'

'Oh Rugger, I understand the dresses now. You are off to the rugger match, top ho. If I was a bit younger, I would give you a ride all the way to London.' She looked at Paul in the rear-view mirror as she said the words. Finn watched as suddenly Paul leaned forward and touched the old lady's arm.

'Yes Jane, all three of us are off to the rugger.' Jane Fetherington turned around with a look of confusion.

'Three, oh dear have we left someone behind?' Paul triumphantly pulled the urn from the plastic bag and placed it on the empty passenger seat beside her.

'This is our mate Big Tony. The daft bastard wrapped himself around a tree back home. We are taking him to watch us fuck the English at Wembley.'

(Mary Rose stands on her toes)

The Bentley roared off leaving the two boys to survey the village of Hamford-Slapton. It was not promising. It looked like a picture postcard hamlet, small cottages with lush colourful flower gardens and a handful of shops. Lady Jane had told them that their best bet was to head to the newspaper shop as it opened at 7 a.m. They sat outside and basked in the warm glow of the rising sun while waiting for the shopkeeper to arrive. 'I am fucking starving. As soon as we get something to eat, we shall get a cab to Northampton.' Paul took another deep drag on his cigarette before continuing. 'Plus, I am running out of fags, we need to get more for the journey.' Finn had his serious face on, and Paul knew a lecture was coming.

'Paul, we have exactly eight pounds between us. How the hell are we going to buy food, fags, pay for a taxi and then get train tickets?' His friend did not get a chance to answer as both of them watched the young woman jump out of the car across the street. Finn had never seen anyone so beautiful before. Her golden curls flowed around her face; she was small but perfectly shaped. Finn was in love. The girl walked up to the door without a glance at the boys and then as she turned the key, she looked down at them and smiled. Her face framed perfectly by the sun shining behind her.

'I like your skirts. I don't think I have ever seen a real Scotsman in Hamford-Slapton before. My name is Mary Rose Chedington. I take it you are waiting for me to open the shop?'

They followed her into the little store and waited as she fussed around getting the place ready. Paul went into his usual charm mode while Finn stood in the background.

'My name is Paul and my shy little friend behind me is called Stumpy. Do you sell sandwiches Miss Chedington or anything to eat and is there a taxi number and a phone box?' The girl burst out laughing. She looked Paul squarely in the eye, she was more than a match for the brazen Scotland fan.

'You have more chance of a man giving birth than finding a taxi in this village. The only thing I sell is newspapers, sweets, and chocolate. But I can see you two boys are suffering so I am happy to share my breakfast with you.' She opened a pack of sandwiches and spread them out on the counter before walking passed Paul and over to Finn.

'What is your real name?' She held her hand out and Finn clasped it gently in his. She felt warm, different, she felt real. They held the handshake for a few seconds before Finn stuttered out his name.

The boys sat on the floor of the shop for the next two hours and talked while the occasional customer came in to buy a newspaper. They would look at the two young men suspiciously, but Mary Rose's infectious smile would tell them everything was ok. The bus for Northampton left outside the shop at 9 a.m. It would get them to the town at 10. Paul had calculated that they would have just enough money left to get train tickets to London. If everything went to plan, they would be meeting Jake at Wembley just before kick-off. What could possibly go wrong?

Paul was already outside watching anxiously for the bus to arrive. Finn did not want to leave the shop. He watched Mary Rose stretch up on her toes to put some packets on a shelf and walked around to help her. 'Let me get that for you.' She turned and laughed.

'Are you trying to tell me I am too small?' Finn's face reddened even though he knew she was just kidding him.

'No, no you are the perfect height. Anyway, I am not exactly a big guy myself.' He took the packets from her hand and reached to place them on the shelf, their bodies momentarily touching. Finn could sense her staring at him. He turned his head and their eyes met. Miss Chedington took his face in her hands and kissed him.

'Finn, Finn, fucking move it. It's time to go, get your arse into gear.' Paul grabbed his friend's arm and pulled him out of the door. He was desperately trying to shout something to Mary Rose as she watched him leave but the moment was gone. He looked for the bus but could not see it.

'Where is the fucking bus Paul, why the panic. It is not even here yet.' Paul continued to drag him across the road towards the Bentley. The one that Lady Jane Fetherington had just left to go and meet her friend, Lord Huxley Stimpy Brown for a coffee. In the confusion Finn found himself sitting in the passenger seat while Paul revved the engine. The large car moved slowly out from the side of the road and moments later it was heading for Northampton.

'Paul what the fuck are you doing. This is fucking insane. What happened to the bus?'

'Fuck the bus. This is quicker. I watched the silly old

cow park up and she left her keys in it. How could we turn down such an opportunity? We deserve a break and this my friend is fucking it.'

'Paul, we will end up in fucking jail you nutcase.'

'Big Tony, will you tell this guy to stop bloody moaning. We are not stealing the car, merely borrowing it. We shall dump it in Northampton and be on the train before she finishes her fucking cake.'

(Dust in the wind)

'Red, red, it's fucking red. You are supposed to stop.' The large Bentley charged across the junction and by some miracle made it to the other side. Finn's face was ashen white. His friend had been fine driving along the lonely country road but now they were in the suburbs of Northampton, things had become dangerous.

'If you had a fucking license you could have driven, but you don't so shut up.' Paul looked flustered. He was finding the old Bentley a lot harder to handle than he expected.

'You don't have a license either you fucking nutcase. Two lessons that you cocked up does not mean you can drive a car, Paul. Red light, watch, watch, another fucking red light.'

'Three, it was three lessons I had. It was not my fault that the instructor was bloody useless.'

They finally agreed to leave the car in a side street and walk the rest of the way to the station. As Paul jumped out of the driver's seat, he patted the bonnet of the Bentley while holding Big Tony in the other arm.

'Good girl, you wait here, and I am sure Mrs. Fetherington will come and find you.' Finn shook his head and both boys started running in the direction of the train station. Paul was taller and fitter and soon left Finn trailing in his desperation to make the next train to London.

Finn slowed down to a walking pace. His head was buzzing, a jumble of emotion and confusion. Wembley, Big Tony's ashes, Paul, Jake, Hamford-Slapton and then he thought of her. Mary Rose, Mary Rose Chedington. Suddenly he laughed out loud, a crazy insane roar of laughter as he ambled up the stairway into Northampton Train station.

Paul was standing on the platform under a sign that said, Trains to London and the South. Big Tony's urn was placed carefully beside him on the ground. He was smiling. 'We made it Finn; we are going to fucking Wemberlee. Me, you, Jake and Big Tony. The four musketeers.' He could see that Finn was not joining in with him in his moment of triumph.

'I don't want to go anymore, Paul. The only reason I am doing this is for you and him.' He pointed at the urn as he spoke.' Paul looked at his friend, a feeling of sadness starting to wash over him. the sudden realisation that everything was changing.

'Look, Finn, you will feel better once we get to London. Let's buy our tickets, we might even have enough money left for a few cans of lager. Mind you, I am not sure what shit the English drink, it won't be Tennent's, that's for certain.' Finn nodded unenthusiastically.

'Yes, whatever you say, Paul.'

Suddenly the roar of an approaching train could be heard in the distance. The noise of screeching metal drowning out their voices. Paul jumped into action, waving his arms above the din.

'Fuck me, quick, we need tickets. The office is this way.'

'It is a fucking goods train, calm down Paul. It is not our train, and it is not stopping.'

The two boys backed away from the edge of the platform as the massive diesel engine roared into sight.

Behind it came a line of clanking coal trucks on their way to some distant power station. Black Dust was flying from the wagons as the train thrashed through Northampton at speed. They watched in amazement as the backdraft from the flying ensemble whipped along the platform, heading straight for Big Tony's urn. Within seconds the container pitched over and was dragged onto the track in the train's wake. As it bounced along underneath the rattling wagons a sea of ashes rose like a Phoenix before finally scattering in the wind.

Paul stood at the edge of the platform looking down at the railway line. The urn had been crushed and its contents emptied back into the earth. Finn walked up to stand by his friend's side. 'Well, you did it this time Paul. No way is Big Tony making it to Wembley for the Scotland game now.' Paul continued to stare at the catastrophe before calmly taking out his packet of cigarettes and lighting one up.

'It is all for the best Finn. Maybe this was supposed to happen.' He inhaled deeply on the cigarette and turned to his friend.

'We only have three tickets; Tony was never going to get in anyway.' Finn shook his head in remembrance of his departed friend as Paul continued to speak.

'We have done him a favour. Ok, I know Big Tony will be pissed that we laid him to rest in fucking England but even that must be better than spending the rest of your life with Big Isobel.'

(England 1 Scotland 2)

They sat on the bench in silence. Neither of them wanted to start talking, they both knew the time had come. Paul finally turned to look at his friend. He poked him in the arm, a last token of affection but even that felt alien now.

'You are not coming with me are you Finn?' Paul looked resigned, a sad glint in his eyes.

'No Paul, it's over. I don't need to go now that Big Tony is dead.' Paul nodded his head in response.

'Are you going back to Coatbridge?' It was a pointless question as he knew the answer already. The two boys stood up and Finn placed his arms around his childhood friend.

'Goodbye Paul. I won't be going back to Coatbridge. I have no reason to. I might stay here; I might not, who knows.' They looked into each other's eyes for a few seconds more and then Finn walked off. Back in the direction, they had come from. Paul remained seated on the bench for a further ten minutes, tears trickling down his face. Finally, he stood up and walked to the booking office. A few minutes later he was walking over the bridge to the opposite platform. The one that said, Trains to Birmingham and The North. In one hand he held a lit cigarette, in the other a ticket back to Glasgow.

(A piece of Wembley turf)

The tartan army was in full song. The march on London had seen an emphatic victory both on the pitch and off. The final whistle signalling a 2-1 win was celebrated in triumph as hordes of Scotland fans invaded the sacred turf. Young men decked in saltires and Tartan swarmed over the green grass of England's national stadium. The goalposts came crashing down under the weight of the marauding Scots. Lumps of grass were ripped from the pitch to be taken back as souvenirs. It was to be a defining moment in Scotland's footballing history. To most, it would never be as good as this again. The following year the aura of world domination was to end in humiliation at the 1978 World Cup in Argentina. For the estimated 60,000 Scots who made the journey to London that day, it would be an experience of a lifetime.

Three miles away from the stadium lay one young man who almost made it. Instead, he lay asleep in a pool of his own vomit. A few hours earlier three fellow supporters had walked over to stare down at him. The crowd was milling past on their way to Wembley, a chorus of *Jimmy Hill's a poof* in full swing. Jake was one of a number who had succumbed to overindulging. One of the men looked as though he was trying to help the unconscious boy up but in reality, he was rifling through his pockets. Five minutes later three ticketless Scotland supporters were standing in stunned silence at their good fortune. The men then started to jump around in a circle while holding on to each other and shouting. We are going to WEMBERLEEEEE.

WHAT A CLEVER
BABY

It was hard to describe the emotions Mavis felt as she trundled along in the green Ford Fiesta. She had never expected to feel this way again. It was now more than 23 years since she had given birth to her only child. Those first few years with Emma had been magical, mother and child in that tight bubble, totally consumed with each other. Of course, every day, every minute she had spent bringing her daughter up had been a joy. It was just that Mavis missed the wonder and innocence a toddler brings in those first few years of flowering. When Emma moved away after finishing her degree, Mavis felt part of her purpose in life had been stolen away. She was proud of her daughter, she had grown into a confident, professional young woman. Mother and daughter still held that special bond, but distance and maturity left Mavis with space she longed to fill.

But now that feeling was back. The elation of being

wanted, held in awe, loved for just being herself. Mavis had been so lucky to have even one child and with only one younger sister she had given up any hope of being called for duty as an aunt. And yet, here she was getting the chance to do it all over again. It had to be a miracle. Jennifer had married late, in her mid-thirties with little expectation of starting a family. She was 42 when the baby arrived, bringing with it all the health fears associated with being an older mother. And yet, she was here, a little whirlwind of golden curls at eighteen months. A bundle of joy, so that was what Jennifer named her, Joy.

The feeling of dizzy excitement was washing over Mavis as she turned the car into Letham Drive. The summer sun glinted off the windscreen, the brightness adding to the elation that poured through her body. Another 100 yards around the bend and they would be waiting. The appointed time had arrived. Jennifer would be trying to hold Joy back as the toddler jumped with excitement at the sight of the slow-moving green cannister edging along the road towards them. Mavis had barely opened the door before the little girl with her mother in tow was grabbing her with delight and excitement.

'One, two, three, oops a daisy.' Both Jennifer and Mavis

aped the words as Joy placed the coloured blocks on top of each other and then knocked them over before repeating the game. The floor of the living room was scattered with soft toys and bits of plastic.

'She really is the cleverest baby that I have ever known. Her speech is coming along so fast.' Jennifer said the words while she watched her little offspring with pride. Of course, her sister had heard others say this and she had said the same about Emma when she had been that age. The two women knew every parent felt that way about their child, but they played along with the charade anyway.

'Oh, she is, absolutely no doubt about it. Only yesterday she was telling me all about the Teletubbies and which one was which.' As if to respond to the conversation, little Joy held up one of the blocks for her aunt.

'Brick, brick, brick.' She handed the plastic block to Mavis before staggering away in that haphazard fashion shared by drunks and toddlers.

Jennifer started to put on her coat. 'I shall only be about an hour Mave. She won't need anything to eat until I get back. Just enjoy playing with her, the way you always do.' The two women laughed as Mavis carried the little girl in her arms to the door to say cheerio to her mother.

'Ta tar, Jo-jo. Mummy will be back soon. Bring you, sweeties, yes my little darling mummy bring you sweet, sweets.'

'Mama, sweet sweets, Mama sweet sweets.' Joy mimicked the words as best as she could at that age. The door closed behind Jennifer as Mavis bounced back into the living room with the little one bobbing up and down and giggling along with her aunt.

The hour passed so quickly. Mavis kept her niece amused by playing games and singing songs. She knew her sister would be back soon, and she would have to hand the little one's attention and affection back to her mother. For some reason, Mavis started to sing the nursery rhyme, Jack and Jill. Maybe it was because she assumed it would be too old fashioned for the toddler to have heard before. It was only as she mouthed the words that Mavis realised how odd it sounded against the modern children's TV programmes such as, The Night Garden and The Teletubbies.

'Jack and Jill went up the hill, to fetch a pail of water. Jack fell down and broke his crown and Jill came tumbling after.' Mavis had become so lost in singing the words that she did not realise that little Joy had stopped playing and was standing shakily in front of her, looking at her auntie in surprise. The toddler's reaction shocked Mavis, she was worried that the words might have frightened the little one.

'Aww, it is ok Jo-Jo, auntie Mavis a silly lady fwightening little Jo-Jo with the silly old nursery rhyme.' Mavis stood up from the sofa before bending down so that her face was only a foot away from little Joy. Slowly the toddlers look of surprise started to recede and her tiny little lips opened to say something.

'What is it little Jo-Jo, what do you want to say to your silly old aunt?'

'Mavis, why did Jack climb up a fucking great hill to get water?', Mavis staggered back in total shock at the words so perfectly announced from the mouth of the little child. 'I mean, why did he not just get a bottle of water from the fucking fridge?'

Bobby lay with his back against the stacked pillows, a set of reading glasses perched on the end of his nose. His eyes strained to read the words of the paperback book he held in one hand. Beside him, Mavis too was supposed to be reading but her eyes stared straight ahead. She had not moved one page in the twenty minutes since they had arrived in the bed. 'Mave, are you going to read that book or just sit staring like a ghost at the wall?' Bobby said the words in a disinterested and resigned tone while continuing to eat up the pages of the spy novel he was reading.

'I know you think I am crazy Bobby but I…oh I just don't understand it.' Bobby sighed and placed his book down on the bed.

'Mave, for heaven's sake, we have been over this a hundred times. It is all you have talked about since coming back from Jen's yesterday. Will you stop acting so bloody daft and get a grip of yourself. If anyone hears you talking like this, they will come to bloody well lock you up.' Mavis turned to her white-haired husband with sadness in her eyes.

'Bobby, do you think I am getting Alzheimer's or maybe going senile?'

'I think you should maybe lay off the drink again for a while Mave. I mean…look I am not stupid. I can tell you are even having a glass of wine before you drive over to Jen's. What if you have an accident? I mean, how much of a warning do you need, woman. Bloody eighteen-month-old kids talking like twenty-year-olds, what the hell next, talking fucking dogs, cats that sing? Honest to Christ woman, get a hold of yourself.' Mavis continued to stare at her husband. She was used to his rants, she simply ignored him and charged on with trying to rationalise what had happened.

'Do you think it is possible that she just heard someone say that and repeated it word for word?' Bobby slowly removed his reading glasses and turned to look at her. For a few seconds, they stared in silence into each other's eyes before he broke the spell.

'I am going to tell you something Mave, and you better listen. Either you stop drinking or you will end up losing contact with your sister and little Joy. You know damn well that the baby did not say those words. It is you and the bloody wine. Is that what you want, to lose touch with the little girl you love so much and who loves you?' Suddenly Mavis was crying. The words from Bobby had finally got through. It was her that was the problem, not the imaginary talking toddler. Mavis turned away as if ashamed of herself.

'You are right Bobby; you are always right. I promise I will stop drinking. How on earth could I even think something so ridiculous and horrible about little Jo-Jo? Oh God, I love that little child, she is like a daughter to me.' Her husband reached down to retrieve his book and shook his head.

'Lost the bloody page I was reading now.'

Mavis stood over the sink, a scouring brush in one

hand and a dinner plate in the other. She sang as she worked away at the dishes. 'Jack and Jill went up the hill to fetch a pale of water, Jack fell down and broke his crown and Jill came tumbling after.' She chuckled to herself as she finished the rhyme. *How could I have been so silly? Poor little Jo-Jo, Bobby was right. I shall stop drinking altogether. What a fool I have been to let alcohol poison my brain.*

The phone in the living room rang. Mavis was too set in her ways to progress to a mobile despite her husband, daughter, and sister Jennifer offering to buy her one. *What would I want with one of those hand thingy phones? They are far too complicated to use. A phone should be on a table, in the house.* She skipped towards the sound coming from along the hall. Mavis knew it would be Jennifer, she called her older sister every day. Tomorrow Mavis would be driving over to look after little Joy for a few hours. The whole saga she had imagined had been put to the back of her mind. She wanted to forget about it, get rid of the shame she felt.

'Hello, hello, is that you Jen?'

'Hi Mave, how are you? You will never guess what little Joy has just said?' Mavis dropped the phone in shock and staggered backward, almost toppling over and into the wall. The phone swung from the coiled wire as it dangled from the edge of the table it usually rested on. The crackling voice of Jennifer could just be made out coming through the earpiece.

'Mave, Mave, are you ok. What has happened? Mave, Mave.' Mavis tried to recover and grabbed the handset. She felt dizzy and sick with fear.

'What did she say, what did she say?' At the other end of the line, Jennifer was holding the phone in disbelief. She could not understand why her older sister was almost screeching the words in a high-pitched voice. Jennifer was almost crying as she tried to reply.

'She just said, Aunt Mave, Aunt Mave, that was all. She was just excited when I told her you were coming over today. In the name of heaven Mave, what is wrong, why are you in such a panic?' Mavis suddenly realised she had made a fool of herself again and had to react quickly to retrieve the situation. She grabbed the phone cable and hauled the handset up to her face.

'Oh, sorry Jen, what an idiot I am. When I heard the phone ring, I got so excited knowing it would be you and little Jo-Jo that I ran to pick it up. I tripped on the carpet and banged my leg.' She could sense that Jenifer was not convinced as she took a while to respond.

'Mave, have you been drinking again?'

'What, oh don't even ask me that Jen. Of course, I have not been drinking, I stopped that years ago. I would never even dream of having a drink, not when I have my little lady to look after. You know I care so much for you both, Jen.'

The two-woman talked for a further five minutes, the conversation ending with neither of them feeling comfortable. Mavis got to talk with Joy who spoke in that half sense language that toddlers have as they try to assemble new words into some kind of order. Jen put her mobile phone on the kitchen table and frowned. She stood thinking for a few minutes and then shrugged her shoulders before bending down to mouth some words to Joy. 'Auntie Mave Mave coming over to see you tomorrow Jo-Jo, Auntie Mave come to see you.' The little girl held out her hand and mimicked, 'Aunt Mave, Aunt Mave.' Meanwhile, seven miles down the road Mavis wiped the sweat from her forehead. She was still shaking from having made such a fool of herself once again. She reached into the cupboard underneath the sink and pulled out the strategically hidden bottle of wine before taking a long swig. Just to calm her nerves of course.

That evening, Jennifer was buzzing around the kitchen. Little Joy was following her every move, mimicking the actions of her mother at work. Stephen would be home from his shift at the Fire Station any minute now and she was desperate to complete cooking the surprise dinner for him. Eating real food was understandably a rare event in the house. Like most couples, once the first baby arrives, life changes dramatically. Less sleep, microwave dinners, and a house turned upside down. Things had become even harder now that Jennifer was back working part-time. For some reason, she felt she had to show Stephen how much she appreciated him. Maybe it was a feeling of guilt as they had so little time together now. He was a great father, husband and he was a fireman, what more could she have asked for?

Stephen was bouncing little Joy into the air and rubbing his face into his daughter as she screamed and giggled with excitement. He stopped for a moment and looked at Jennifer as her arms reached into the oven. 'So, tell me why tonight is so special then Jen. It can't be our anniversary; it is not my birthday and I am sure it is not yours. Let me think, nope definitely not your birthday as that is January 12th.' Jennifer laughed as she carried the tray of steaming hot pasta towards the well-set dining table.

'Pack it in Steph, you know damn well my birthday is June 2nd. And I don't need a reason to treat my wonderful husband other than to let him know I love him. Put Jo-Jo into the highchair and park your bottom at the table. Would you like a glass of wine?'

'You know what Jen? For once I am going to have a little drink, today was hard going. We had that bloody training day thing again, all climbing and carrying. I am bloody whacked. There is something I really fancy?' Jennifer started to ladle the food out onto the plates while Joy banged enthusiastically on the front of the highchair with her plastic spoon.

'What is it you want and whatever it is could you get it while I feed Jo-Jo, or we will not get five minutes to eat this pasta.'

'I am going to have a whisky. I shall open that bottle your sister Mavis got me for Christmas, one drink will be enough.' Jennifer laughed.

'Whisky, on a school night. Jesus, you must have had a tough day. The only time you touch that stuff is new year along with that bloody awful cigar you insist on smoking.' She lifted the plastic spoon and tried to place the food into Joy's mouth. As usual, more of it spilled onto her bib than went where it should have. Stephen was opening the kitchen cabinet and reaching inside for the bottle of whisky.

'I only smoke a cigar once a year, it was a tradition my dad used to have. You want a shot of this stuff Jen?'

'Are you kidding? Pour me a glass of white wine. Whisky reminds me of petrol and hurry up before your pasta goes cold.' Stephen did not reply but was standing holding the bottle of whisky up to his face, as if he was staring the label.

'Jen.' His wife did not look up as she continued the battle to get the toddler to eat. Most of it was spilling on the tray at the front of the highchair. Joy was making it clear that she had no interest in eating the mush her mother was feeding her. Suddenly Jennifer became aware that Stephen was silent. She turned to see him holding the bottle close to his eyes, studying it with a look of confusion on his face.

'Stephen, what the hell are you doing? This dinner I spent so long making is going to go cold. Are you going to open that bottle or stare at it all night?' Her husband turned around to face her, holding the whisky for Jennifer to see with his outstretched arm.

'It's been opened, Jen. In fact, it is half empty. I can tell you for sure, it was not me. Have you been drinking my petrol?' Jennifer frowned, a look of sadness in her eyes.

'You know damn well it was not me Stephen. But I

know who it must have been.'

Mavis was spinning little Jo-Jo in her daddy's office swivel chair. The little girl giggled with excitement as she twirled round and round. The toddler's mood was the polar opposite to that of the two women in the house. Mavis had taken Joy into her father's room so that she would not see that her mum had been crying. Jennifer had promised herself that she would confront her sister about her drinking again but do it in a calm manner. Of course, it did not go that way. As soon as she had approached the subject, Mavis had become defensive. The older sister had vehemently denied that she had fallen off the wagon. Jennifer had quickly lost her cool and it had descended into a shouting match. Only when Little Jo-Jo started crying did the two sisters realise things had gone too far. After the fall out comes the making up. Mavis had finally broken down and admitted her old alcohol habits had returned. The two women hugged and cried. The hoped-for reconciliation had come when Mavis agreed she would always take a home alcohol test if she was left alone with her little niece.

Jennifer walked into the office. It was still obvious that she had been crying but hopefully, the toddler would not get upset now that the two women had calmed down.

Mavis gave the swivel chair a big push as Joy continued to giggle and bounce up and down on the seat. The emotion in her voice still showed as she made one last protestation of innocence.

'Jen, I swear to God that...' Her sister jumped in before they ended up going down the same road again.

'Mave, stop. We have agreed. There is no more need to talk about it. You have admitted you are drinking again. There is nothing I can do about that, but it is black and white from now on. You take an alcohol test if you are watching Joy and we will make sure there is no drink left around the house.' Mavis looked at her younger sister with resignation. She felt utterly defeated as well as humiliated.

'I was just going to say. I admit I have been drinking wine, not a lot, just enough to keep my nerves calm. But I swear Jen, I swear to God, I did not drink Stephens whisky.' Jennifer held up her hand to signal the conversation was over.

'It no longer matters Mave. I love you and I want you to continue the amazing relationship you have with my daughter. You do the test each time and that keeps both of us happy.' Little Joy had stopped spinning and was now looking up at her favourite auntie.

'Spin, spin, Mav Mav, spin, spin.' The little girl's innocent words broke the tension between the two women, and both burst out laughing.

'What a clever little girl you are Jo-Jo.' Mavis bent down and kissed the toddler on the head before pushing the chair into a twirl one again.

Mavis steered the car into the driveway of her house. She had completed the ride home on autopilot. One of those trips when you cannot remember a single thing about the actual journey. The voices in her head had gone on the attack. *What will Bobby say if he finds out? This is exactly what he said would happen. Jen was wrong to accuse me of stealing Stephens whisky; I would never do that. A few glasses of wine, that was all. Bloody hell everyone else is allowed a little drink every now and then. I never touched his bloody whisky, I don't even like the stuff.*

It was only the incessant ringing of the phone that cleared the clutter battling inside her brain. Mavis hurriedly pushed the key into the door. 'Oh, for heaven's sake come on, come on.' Her agitation to get into the house before the caller rang off only caused her to waste more time as the key jammed in the lock. She finally managed to calm down and once inside she ran to the living room to grab the phone.

'Hello, Mavis here how can I he…'

'Mave, Mave, you need to come back. Oh God, you need to get back here quickly.' A cold sweat rushed through Mavis's body as she listened to the panic in her younger sister's voice.

'Jen, what is it, what is it?'

'It's Stephen, there has been some sort of accident at work. I don't know what it is. Oh Jesus, Mave, please get over here as quick as you can. I need you to look after Joy for me. Please hurry.'

Mavis steered the car around the corner of Letham Drive. This arrival would be different than any other. Jennifer was already standing in the doorway with her coat on. She started to run to her own car as soon as Mavis pulled up. 'Mave, no time to talk, I need to go. Jo-Jo is watching TV in Stephen's office. I will call you at the house as soon as I hear anything.' Jennifer was already driving away before her sister had reached the doorway of the house. A voice in her head was saying, *well the alcohol test rule did not last for long, did it, Mavis?* She tried to clear her mind and get rid of the guilt she felt for even thinking that way. *Stop that Mavis, poor Stephen is laying in the hospital, anything could have happened.*

She walked along the hall, passed the living room and onwards to the office with the swivel chair. 'Jo-Jo, you watching the Tel-Tel, auntie Mav-Mav is here.' She mimicked the words in that high-pitched fashion family keep for young children. The sort of voice that would get you locked up if you used it when talking to adults. Mavis could see the back of the swivel chair that faced the television. Little Joy's tiny frame completely hidden in the large seat. But something was wrong, Mavis stood frozen in the doorway of the office. Unable to move. Smoke was rising from the chair, wisps of smoke curling slowly in haphazard white patterns towards the ceiling. A distinct aroma filled the room. The only time Mavis could remember smelling it before had been during Christmas in this very house.

Slowly she took control of her senses and the creeping dread that was enveloping her whole body. Step by step Mavis edged towards the chair, sweat running down her forehead and dripping onto the carpet. Her hand reached out to touch the back of the swivel chair, her fingers making contact with the cold leather. Then inch by inch she pushed the frame around until she looked in horror upon the tiny child sitting facing her. In one hand little Jo-Jo held a lit cigar, in the other a tiny plastic tumbler filled with whisky. The almost empty bottle stood on the desk beside the television. The little girl threw her head back before slowly blowing a smoke ring that went curling upwards.

'Mavis, tell me again. Why did Jack climb that fucking great hill when he could have got water from the fridge? I mean, was he fucking retarded or something?'

SPRING (RANDOM ACTS OF VIOLENCE)

This must be the season of hope. The black winter is fading as the first signs of life start to emerge from the frozen ground. We face towards the light while behind us the dark cowers as it descends into shadow.

Have you ever heard someone say, *I loved school, they are the best days of your life?* The speaker will often have a wistful sentimental look. Their eyes gazing into the distance at the happy thoughts of being the lead in the school panto, captaining the school football team or just remembering the funny japes they got up to in the playground. Smiling running children all helping each other through those difficult years of adolescence. Well, let me put something straight, right now. That is not how I remember it, not by a long way. No sir, no fucking way.

I spent my school years during the sixties and seventies in the West of Scotland. If I am being honest, I would have to say I did not live in one of the tougher areas of Glasgow. The Southside could be considered as reasonably affluent but that made little difference in the world of children and teenagers. This was long before multiculturalism, inclusion, equality, and respect became part of the curriculum. There were two ways to survive, either fight it out or work hard at staying under the radar. I chose the latter. Not because I am a coward. It is just that I barely reach five foot six now, in those day's it was a lot less. Oh, and the sight of blood made me feel faint. Even more so if it was mine. Bullying was an everyday occurrence; you both received it and gave it out. Everyone was bullied, by whom just depended on where you sat in the hierarchy. Now I hear you ask, *what about the teachers, could you not go to them for help?* No chance, they also fit into the bullying hierarchy. Weak teachers would be tormented by the pupils, strong teachers would wield the belt like King Arthur with his sword.

Looking back, I can measure my school years by the random acts of violence I witnessed. In my first year at Secondary school, I stood in a queue behind two older boys waiting to buy junk food in the morning break. In those days they had someone selling crisps and chocolate out of one of the lower windows of the building. The peddling of such an unhealthy product would not be allowed in the modern age of course but oddly, everyone was as thin as a rake. If by chance you were the rare exception to this rule, then God help you. Being called Billy Bunter would be the least of your problems.

Anyway, back to the two big guys in front of me. Everyone was big to me of course. The window they sold stuff out of had a concrete ledge at the bottom, it would be just about at head height for the taller ones. The boy at the front had his face just inches from the ledge when his friend, yes, his friend, simply pushed his face into the ledge. This was done for no other reason than he thought it was funny. The boy's face smashed into the concrete, his broken teeth hanging from the blood pouring out of his mouth. 'What the fuck did you do that for?' The other boy just laughed. And you know the most amazing thing? The woman serving just ignored it all and moved onto the next in line. That was me but by this point, I no longer fancied the packet of tomato crisps I was intending to buy with my school dinner money. I left quickly; all my teeth still intact.

That same year a new boy came to our school after the term had started. That would have been bad enough for him because by then everyone had found their place in the pecking order. So, unless the newcomer was a champion boxer, he was fucked. Sadly, for the new kid on the block not only was he from South Africa, but his parents had also committed the worst sin imaginable on their poor child. They had let him come to secondary school with short trousers on. Now, this might have been ok in Johannesburg but in the early seventies Scotland! Oh dear. The poor soul spent each break period having his legs spat on by every other pupil he went near. Again, I am sure the teachers saw all this, but they did nothing. The next day he arrived with long trousers, but it was too late, they still did the same. I could lie and say I befriended him but like I mentioned, I was trying to survive under the radar.

Occasionally I would get noticed and it would be my turn to get picked on. One of the nutcases used verbal torture on me. He would taunt me about fancying the best-looking girl in the class. Of course, it was ridiculous, the good-looking girls did not give me a second look, the not so good-looking ones didn't either. I finally cracked one day and as he walked past mimicking my voice, I pushed my desk into him. I think I overdid it as It nearly broke his leg. He got back up and slammed the desk back into me while I was still seated. Despite it almost making me into a hospital case he did leave me alone after that. Maybe I had gained a little respect.

I could recount endless acts of violence; it was an everyday occurrence. The hard man chased across the playground by a gang with bricks. They smashed one over his head. The boy who was hung out of the third-floor window ledge, held precariously by another two pupils. The incident in the Chemistry lab when someone placed a lit Bunsen burner underneath a boy's coat, while he was wearing it. He survived with minor burns. The lethal firework rockets that would screech down the corridor bouncing off the walls. All of this would be met with the weary threat from the teachers of retribution if they caught the culprits. They never did, I think they just hid in the staff room and allowed the carnage to run unabated around them.

You officially ended your school days once the summer started. I finally walked away one day in Spring. I had probably given up long before then. I stepped out into the big bad world wondering if things could get any worse. I thought that school had taught me nothing, but I was wrong. It gave me the gift of being able to survive. I found working so much easier. Away from the bullying culture people turned out to be quite nice. I am sure many of you enjoyed your school days and it would be wrong of me to say I have no happy memories. I have one, it was that Spring day when I left.

BLIND DATE WITH
TUNNEL VISION

(Floating words)

Colin fidgeted nervously at the front door of 26 Byron Crescent. He had a forlorn hope that his brother Robert would not be home even though he knew with absolute certainty that the shuffling figure would answer the door. The weekly visit to see his sibling had become the one thing in life that Colin dreaded. It had been so different when Karen was alive, her infectious enthusiasm had radiated from every inch of the building. No matter what time or what day you called, she would welcome you with innocent affection and open arms. Robert would be close behind. Was he a misery even then? Maybe Karen's positive aura had simply surrounded her husband so that you did not notice him. The more Colin thought about it, the harder it was to remember what his brother had been like when his wife was with him. It was as if he only started to exist as a person once Karen had passed away.

He could see the shadow ambling to the door. The frosted glass twisting Roberts silhouette into a shimmering ghost. Colin had even changed his weekly visit to a Wednesday evening rather than a Monday, in the hope that his brother might not be home. Everything about Robert was a losing battle. *Why would he not be home? He never went out*, Colin knew that. His brother would wake up, go to work at eight and be home by six. Other than that, he would be inside the four walls of 26 Byron Crescent, eating, sleeping and existing. The rattle of the chain and the sliding of the latch heralded Colin's weekly torture as the door opened.

Robert did not even look at his brother, he knew who it would be. No one else visited him except for the few unfortunate cold callers who would usually have the door slammed in their face. 'Hello Rob, it is me Colin, your brother. Wow, I can see you are pleased to see me.' The words were said with a heavy tone of sarcasm.

'Look, Colin. I don't ask you to visit. You come because you feel obliged to, or guilty. I have no fucking idea why you bother. Do you want a cup of tea?'

'I come to see you because you are my brother, Rob. That is what brothers do. Anyway, Jane makes me come. She worries about you.'

'The only reason Jane asks you to keep seeing me is that she loved Karen so much. Everybody did. Everybody did, oh fuck I miss her so much Colin.' His voice started to break with emotion, memories wrapping themselves around each word. Robert stopped filling the kettle and placed his hands on the sink, his head bent, looking down. A study in dejection. Colin walked up close to his brother and placed a weary hand on his shoulder. He was going through the act; this happened every time he visited. The same speech, the same broken man, refusing to even attempt to get out of the mire.

'Robert, Robert, you have to stop this. It has been almost five years. Five long years, you have to move on. This is crazy. Karen would have hated to see you like this. Look, we all loved her, and I know you miss her. But fucking hell brother, this is just giving up. Is that what you want?' Robert turned to face his younger sibling, the glint of tears in his eyes.

'I don't want to be like this Colin, I really don't. It is just, oh God I miss her so much. Every second, everything I do. It just feels empty, I have nothing, I feel nothing. Maybe if we had been able to have children, I would at least have had something, someone to share this grief with.'

'You need to get out Rob, meet other people. Find someone who feels like you. Maybe another woman who also lost her partner? I know it is hard, but you need to get back in the marketplace. I know it sounds ridiculous but maybe it would give you something to look forward to, a challenge.' Robert laughed, not a happy laugh but one that sounded empty, as though the words his brother had uttered had fallen to the ground at his feet.

'Bloody hell Colin. Are you serious? Do you see me going on a date? I look like I have been stuck in a time warp for the last twenty-five years.'

It was nearly eight o'clock, the torture was over for another week. Colin zipped up his jacket as he placed his hand on the door. He turned to look back at his brother as his mouth started to say the words. But he stopped before the sound left his lips. The picture of Robert standing there, worn brown corduroy trousers, a washed-out grey t-shirt under his woollen cardigan, black socks covered by old slippers, told him it would be a waste of time. He said his goodbyes and walked up the path from his brother's house to the car.

The headlights disappeared into the distance leaving the man in the once-proud bungalow alone. The uncut grass, wild bushes, and broken gutters perfectly mirroring the hopelessness that emanated from the building. But even as each man went in their different directions, the words that Colin had said were floating in the air. Slowly seeping back into the house, looking for him, searching him out. *You need to get out Rob, meet other people. Find someone who feels like you. Maybe another woman who also lost her partner? Get back in the marketplace.*

(Back in the marketplace)

The evenings were already growing dark as Autumn descended on the damp ground. Colin stepped out of his car with the usual sense of hopelessness. If it was possible, he felt even worse than he had during his visit only a week before. Maybe it was the final loss of summer, the knowledge that from now on he would be turning up at his brother's house in darkness. The contrast of light and shadow that had helped him get through previous visits would now be gone. The gloom outside would perfectly match the bleakness inside.

He was half-way along the path before he noticed the change. It was so unexpected that Colin had to stop and stare at it to make sure his eyes did not deceive him. The long grass of the once-loved lawn had been cut. It looked brown and cropped, a mess but it did not matter. The fact that it had been mown was all Colin cared about. It was so unusual, the first none-compulsory thing his brother had done since Karen had died. The opening act in the climb back from the pit. Colin rattled the door, for the first time in years he felt a tiny hint of hope in his heart. A minuscule seed to grasp hold of, something to make this visit different from all the others he had endured.

The two men were in their usual positions. Robert bent over the sink filling the kettle, Colin standing nervously at the kitchen table dreading the opening gambit of the dual. One brother trying desperately to steer the conversation away from the dead woman, the other ready to grasp any opportunity to talk about her. 'I see you had the front lawn cut; it looks nice.' The words sounded so ridiculous that Colin could feel his face redden as the blood pumped through his body.

'Yes, I did it when I came home from work yesterday. I

thought it was about time I got up and tried something other than lay in front of the television.' Robert turned around to pour the boiling water into the cups. It was only then than Colin noticed the change in his brother's appearance.

'Wow, nice haircut. Is that you finished with your scruffy hippy period then?'

'Very funny. I just decided to get a trim, my boss told me I need to tidy up a bit, that's all.' Robert carefully poured the milk into the cups before handing one over to his brother and walking off towards the living room. Colin watched him with bemused affection. His brother still wore the same motley collection of clothes and the inside of the house remained unkempt and unloved. But, the subtle change in his brother's appearance, as well as the grass being cut, was totally unexpected and a major step away from the past.

'Wow, a haircut for you and the front garden, all in one week. What the hell happened? Are you feeling ok?' Colin knew he had overstepped the mark as soon as the words came out. He could not help it, Robert always made him feel nervous and awkward.

'Ok, don't fucking go on about it. I, I just wanted to try and take some small steps, well you know? To get over her.'

Colin walked towards his brother and placed his hands on his sibling's shoulders.

'I know Rob, I know. I just want you to find some happiness again.' Just for that few seconds, they entered each other's circle, family again. The barrier was still there but now it had come down in height and the two men could peer over the top and see each other for the first time in years.

The hour passed far quicker than usual as the two men chatted, both being careful not to mention the deceased woman. Of course, her ghost still hovered over the house, listening to the words, filing them for future reference. Colin put his coat on and walked towards the front door, his brother following him to say goodbye. The two men gave each other an awkward embrace and with a perfunctory, *take care, I will see you next week*, He pulled the handle and stepped outside.

'Erm, Colin, Can I ask you something?' This was another step forward for Robert. He never asked for advice, at least not since Karen had died.

'Yes, of course, Rob. What is it?' Robert shuffled awkwardly before responding.

'Well, you know you mentioned last week, that thing.

Well, erm, how do I do it?'

'What thing? I don't know what you mean?' Robert looked uncomfortable but he had to continue now, there was no going back.

'You said that I should, Get back in the marketplace. How do I do that, you know, get back in the marketplace?'

(Lorna)

'Thanks for coming over Colin, I do appreciate it.'

'That is what brothers are for Rob, I am here to help you. Although, I feel we should have got Jane in on this. How the hell am I supposed to know what a 42-year-old man should wear on a date? The last time I went out with a woman was 15 years ago and I ended up marrying her.' Robert adjusted his tie, he felt ridiculous. He had a work shirt on, a sports jacket, jeans, and casual shoes.

'Oh, fuck Colin, I look bloody ridiculous with this tie, it needs to come off. She will think I am meeting her for a fucking interview.' Robert pulled the tie off and continued to fidget with his clothes while looking in the large hallway mirror.

'You know what they say about computer dating sites

don't you Rob?' His brother turned to look at him.

'Go on tell me then Colin, now that you have become such a dating expert.'

'They say it's just for people to meet up and have casual sex.' Both men laughed, Colin because it was funny, Robert because he was feeling nervous. In fact, he was terrified. It had all happened so fast. A few nights spent chatting online after work and he had his first date in what felt like centuries.

'Well, I should be so fucking lucky, Colin. Anyway, Mr. Smart arse, it is not a dating site, it is a social networking site, or something like that. I need to go; how do I look. Is she going to take one glance at me and burst out laughing?' Colin stood back and eyed up his brother as though he was some sort of professional in the dating game.

'You look absolutely stunning darling, Mel Gibson's double.' Robert was already hurrying towards the front door.

'Fuck off Colin. I probably look more like Frankenstein's double.' As Robert disappeared into the night towards his car his brother shouted some words of encouragement.

'Just go and enjoy the experience, Rob. I am just happy that you are getting out and about again. Call me tomorrow and let me know how it goes.'

Robert sat in the Blakewell Arms feeling incredibly self-conscious. This was one of at least a dozen pubs in the dormitory town of Harkendon, chosen because he knew it would be quiet on a Tuesday evening. Robert dreaded the thought that someone he and Karen had known might see him. He felt guilty, an act of disloyalty to his beloved partner even though she had been gone for five years. He scanned the surroundings. Lights flickered from the gaming machine sitting in the corner of the pub, a handful of couples scattered around the large seating area and two men on barstools chatting to the young barmaid. Ten minutes and his date would arrive. His hands clasped the cold pint of lager, but he made no attempt to drink it. This was it, the last chance to run before she arrived.

He knew very little about Lorna. The photographs on the dating site had only shown her upper body. She was slightly older than him, divorced and worked in a primary school. It was only after a few evenings chatting that he had learned she was not a teacher but worked in the canteen. *Who cares, so long as she is sociable and friendly, just enjoy yourself, Robert. You have nothing to lose. If it does not work out, you don't even need to see her again.*

Suddenly he felt a slight rush of cold air brush past

causing him to look at the main door to the bar. It was still closed but it was only then that he noticed her. In a dark alcove at the far end of the large lounge, Robert could make out the shapely legs of a woman. They protruded from the side of a panelled section that held a small sofa. It kept the lonely occupant partially hidden from view, but it was enough to recognise that she was on her own. It seemed strange that a woman would sit by herself on a quiet Tuesday evening, maybe she too was waiting for a date to show. He tried to focus his eyes through the gloom, drawn to the legs, those legs.

'He…hello. I think I recognise you from the photos Robert, I am Lorna, Lorna Stevens. It is nice to meet you.' Robert had been so engrossed in the distant legs that he jumped with fright at the sudden intrusion. His date had appeared from directly behind him. The pint of lager went tumbling across the table spilling its contents over Robert and the floor.

'Oh dear, shall I get you another drink?' Robert stood up to greet her, already feeling like a total fool.

'Sorry, I did not realise there was a back entrance into the pub, you just startled me, that's all.' Lorna gave him a confused look.

'No, I came in through the main door, the one you are facing!'

The date did not get off to the best start and from that point on it floundered. She sat opposite Robert, sipping her diet coke while the two of them tried to make polite conversation. Lorna was a large woman; he tried his best not to compare her to Karen, but it was impossible. His deceased wife had been tall, slim, chatty and full of life. The lady opposite seemed shy and Robert was finding her talk to be dull. It was not her fault. Robert felt distracted, no matter how hard he tried to engage with Lorna, his eyes kept being drawn to the legs sitting in the distance. The date ended within an hour, both participants realising it was going nowhere. Robert tried to be polite and let the charade play itself out. 'Well, it was very nice to meet you, Lorna, maybe we could do this again?' She looked him up and down before replying.

'I don't think so, Robert. If you don't mind me saying, I don't think you are ready to be dating yet. You still talk about your wife a lot and you have a habit of looking over people's shoulders while you talk to them.' Lorna did not take the outstretched hand he offered but simply headed off towards the main door and within seconds she was gone.

Robert was already putting his coat on, all that mattered to him was to see who the legs belonged to. *Walk past her, take a quick glance and then head home.* But when he looked towards the alcove, she had gone. The gloom had descended into the corner while the lights of the gaming machine danced around trying to attract customers that did not exist.

(Briony)

Robert smoothed down his suit as he stood sideways staring into the mirror. His brother watched him with detached amusement.

'I must admit, I am impressed, Rob.'

'Impressed with what, Colin? If you are here to take the piss, then why don't you just fuck off back to Jane and watch Coronation Street on the telly.' Colin ignored the good-natured insult from his brother and continued talking. He was enjoying these visits now, the change in Robert was incredible. He seemed to be growing in confidence each time he came to see him, at long last leaving the past and Karen behind.

'Well, the fact that you are going on another blind date after throwing a pint of beer over the last poor woman you met.' The two men laughed, as Robert took one final full-length look at himself in the mirror.

'It can't go any worse, that is for sure. Anyway, it was me who got soaked, not her. Mind you, she was a real bore, maybe I should have poured it over her.' Colin eyed his brother up with a slight surprise.

'Well, Rob, give this one a chance tonight. Don't judge her straight away, you need to work at developing a relationship.' Robert was already making a move to the front door.

'I know, I know. I will Colin, I am learning.'

'Nice suit, Rob. You certainly are learning, you look, good brother, you really do.'

'Do you think so? Cheers Colin, I am trying to make more of an effort.' The two men parted ways as they left the house and walked to their respective cars. Their feet crunching on the wet leaves that lay scattered over the lawn and the paths. Colin turned to shout a few last words of encouragement as his brother edged into his car.

'I still think you would have been better meeting her somewhere other than that awful Blakewell Arms. It is a dump.' The words floated unheard into the dark evening as Robert turned the ignition and the engine spluttered into life.

He sat at the same table, facing the door. This time his hands were resting on the surface, a few inches of the Lager already consumed. He felt more relaxed, certainly more relaxed than his first date. Briony sounded sweet, their online chat had made him laugh. She had a sharp sense of humour and looked good in the photographs. Robert tried to convince himself that the Blakewell Arms was the best place to meet up. He knew that was not true though. Now he had become slightly more confident he could have arranged to meet in one of the better pubs or even one of the many Harkendon Restaurants. He would not openly admit it, but he was back here because of her. The woman with the legs, the apparition of lust who had sat hidden in the corner. Robert smiled to himself, *for God's sake Rob, grow up. You are on a date tonight, make the best of it and forget your stupid fantasies.*

Briony was walking through the main door but Robert's eyes were already straying to the tables in the distance. There just beneath one of the many big television screens showing that night's football match was the woman. Once again, she sat alone but this time, she faced the screen with her back to Robert. Long blonde hair flowing over her shoulders, bare arms silhouetted against her tight black top. He could not see those legs, but it was not hard to imagine them extended out beneath the table. She was like a magnet to him, he felt like he wanted to gaze upon her forever.

'Robert, Rob, so good to meet you. What a journey I had getting here; you would not believe it. I had to get a number 43A to Clammerford Road and then change to the 17B and get off at Park Street. Then I had to walk half a mile to find this place. And it has started bloody raining, I mean how unlucky is that? But I am here now, can you get me a gin and lemonade my love, in a tall glass with ice and a dash of lime. Ask him to fill the glass to the top with Lemonade, you know what these barmen are like. Oh, and I came straight from work. A packet of salted peanuts would be lovely as well. Did I tell you...'

Robert was glad to get to the bar. Already he knew that Briony was not going to work out. Maybe it was nerves, but she talked nonstop. It had been ok on the computer chat; he had been able to type words while she did the same. She was slim, smaller than he had expected, maybe in her late forties but none of it mattered. He was waiting for the barman to pour the gin and lemonade, trying to not make it look obvious that he wanted to watch her, the lonely woman. The young barman placed the drink and peanuts on the counter, 'Six pounds twenty, please.' Robert handed him ten pounds.

'Who is the woman over by the television? I have seen her a few times; it is odd that she comes in here on her own.' Scott looked over to where Robert's eyes gazed. He said nothing but the barman looked uncomfortable. He handed the change to him and quickly walked away. It was obvious Scott did not want to talk. There were only him, Briony and the woman in the place on this dark and damp Monday evening.

Robert sat for the next hour while Briony talked at him. If he had been listening he would have heard about her ex-husband the alcoholic, her three children, one of them who was already in prison for selling drugs, the problems she was having with the council who had yet to fix the roof and the boiler, her two dogs, the different buses she had used to get here tonight (again) and so on. He just sat and occasionally nodded his head or grunted, *is that so, well I never. That's the bloody council for you.* You will know by now that Robert could not take his eyes off the rolling blonde hair and the smooth bronzed skin, the perfect woman sitting all alone with her back to him.

'Robert, Robert.' The sharp tone of Briony's voice

suddenly pulled him back to his immediate surroundings. It was dawning on him that he could not remember even sitting at this table for the last twenty minutes.

'Oh yes, sorry Briony. Yes, so did the council get your boiler fixed then?' The little woman opposite him was standing. In her anger, she seemed to expand and now towered over Robert who remained seated with his hands clasped around the almost full pint of lager.

'You fucking ignorant son of a bitch. You have been ignoring me all evening, staring into space like some gormless twat. You cheeky sod, I spent ages jumping on different buses to get here and you fucking ignore me. Why the hell did you agree to come on a date, it is bloody obvious that you do not want to be here.' She grabbed the beer glass from Robert's hands and threw the contents into his face. For just a few seconds the shock made his eyes turn away from the distant object of his desire. He watched Briony storm towards the front door of the pub, still talking to herself.

'You fucking big loser, I have had better men than you, real gentlemen. Not big bloody ignoramuses like you.'

The beer was running down his face, stinging his eyes. He desperately tried to rub the liquid away with his hands, but they too were soaked. All he could see was the flickering of the lights from the gaming machine. The on/ off flashing and the dripping lager making it impossible to see her, the woman. Someone handed him a towel. Robert grabbed it with gratitude and wiped his face. Standing in front of him was Scott, the barman. He was grinning, trying desperately not to laugh. Robert stepped to the side so he could see around the young man who now blocked his vision. The television still flashed its moving images of the football match, the gaming machine still blinked its myriad of colourful lights, but she was gone. The chair still faced the same way, but it no longer held the woman of his dreams.

(Danielle or Rayna, will it matter in the end?)

'And you did this for a whole fucking week?' Colin sounded incredulous but nothing surprised him about his brother these days. The changes in Robert had been so dramatic in the last few months that even this latest revelation was not totally unexpected.

'So, you sat in the Blakewell Arms for seven nights in the hope that some woman who you have never met, might turn up?' Robert continued to comb his slick backed hair to style the gel into the shape he wanted.

'It was only three nights, stop fucking exaggerating. Anyway, she was not there. I Know it was daft and a total waste of time.' He spoke the words in that casual manner you would expect from some British B movie film star of the fifties.

'Ok, three nights then. Bloody hell Rob, no wonder that poor woman, what was her name, oh Lorna, threw a pint over you.' Robert placed the comb on the table and squinted his head to the side while he eyed up his profile in the mirror.

'Briony, it was Briony who threw the pint over me. Lorna was the one who accidentally knocked a pint over me. There is a subtle difference.' Colin laughed and shook his head.

'Rob, I really do think you are starting to fancy yourself as some sort of big shot smooth operator. What happened to the meek Rob I used to know? The one who was terrified to leave the house, the one who wore old slippers and a cardigan. I mean, where on earth did you get that new suit from? Will you bloody stop preening yourself in front of the mirror and answer me, Mr. Casanova?' Both men were laughing now. Robert was heading towards the door, his brother once again following in his footsteps.

'Casanova? I bet he never got beer thrown over him. Look, Colin, this is the last date. I think she is going to be the one, I feel it in my bones. The suit is because I intend to really make an impression with her tonight. Even her name, Danielle, it sounds, well it sounds just right.' Robert was putting on his coat, outside the evening frost was speeding Autumn towards the encroaching winter.

'Just promise me one thing then Rob.' His brother was just about to jump into his car.

'Yes, go on Colin. What advice are you going to give me now?'

'Just promise me you will give this new date your full attention and forget any fantasies about strange ladies with great legs.' Robert winked at his brother before pulling the driver's door over.

'Danielle is going to get my full attention. The leg lady is yesterday's fantasy, she is history.'

Robert felt good. He knew he looked cool in his new suit, stylish and elegant, a man growing in confidence. The Blakewell Arms looked the same as it did every evening at the start of a new week. There was a new barman on tonight. He had not seen Scott since the beer throwing incident, not that he cared. Robert was now a ladies man, tonight he would hit the target either way. Danielle sounded like the kind of woman he wanted to get to know, and if it did not work out? Well, she would appear, of course, she would. That was the game, he knew that now. She would only come when he was out on a date.

Maybe this evening was going to be different after all. Danielle was walking towards him and there had been no sign of the woman. She was smiling, casually dressed in jeans but she looked good. He stood up to welcome her, giving his date the full attention, he had promised.

'Robert, I assume it is you?' Both of them laughed as other than the new barman they were the only two occupants of The Blakewell Arms so far this evening.

'Good guess, my name is indeed, Robert. And your name, let me think, would it be Danielle?' They seemed to click straight away. Danielle had a relaxed manner and was interesting as well as being a good listener.

'You look very smart in your suit Robert; I should have made more effort. You are putting me to shame.' He reached out and touched the top of her arm.

'You look amazing Danielle.' She laughed and then tried to be serious.

'There is one thing I should mention Robert. I hope you don't mind but Danielle is not my real name. I give a false name just in case. I have been on a lot of these dates and some of the guys I have met, well let's just say I don't want them to be able to track me down.'

'Oh, well that sounds like a compliment to me then, I mean if you are going to tell me your real name?' This time she touched his shoulder, the bonding was complete.

'Yes, I can tell you are a nice guy Robert. My real name is Rayna.'

The next few hours passed unnoticed as the two of them talked and laughed. They discussed moving on to another pub or going for something to eat but they were so comfortable in each other's company the conversation kept flowing and the move never happened. Which is a pity, because had they left then it might have all worked out a lot better. Robert was looking into Danielle's eyes, chuckling at the story she was telling about her last disastrous date. Behind her, the lights of the gaming machine flickered and flashed. The glow reflected around the edges of Danielle's face, lighting it up in the dim surroundings of The Blakewell Arms. It was this reflected aura that dragged him away from the bubble that enveloped the two of them. A shadow had crept across his vision causing his eyes to search for the reason. She was there, in the distance, her back to him while she slowly placed coins into the gaming machine. A figure-hugging tight black dress, the flowing blonde hair, those legs. He could not take his eyes off her even if he tried. Once again, she had him under control, held in a complete trance.

'Robert, are you ok?' Rayna turned around to look in the same direction as her now inattentive date. He closed his eyes to try and break the spell.

'Yes, yes, I am fine. I, I just thought that was someone I knew.'

'Who? I thought it was the fruit machine you were staring at. We can have a go on it, if you like. I have a few pound coins in my purse.'

'No, no, let her play it. A waste of money in my opinion.' Rayna looked at him, confusion in her eyes.

They talked for another thirty minutes but the bond was broken. Robert tried desperately to get things back on track, but his eyes would betray him as they darted between Danielle and the woman at the machine. The crunch point came when the apparition in the black dress picked up the handbag that she had placed at her feet. She was leaving, but this time Robert had no intention of letting her out of his grasp again. He jumped up just as she disappeared through the main entrance of the Blakewell Arms.

'Oh, what is wrong Robert. Is it something I said or did? Have I offended you?' Tears were started to well in Rayna's eyes. She could not understand how things had gone so wrong when they had felt so right just thirty minutes before. She was certain that they had clicked, he was funny, charming, smartly dressed. What had changed? It all started when he suddenly became distracted, staring as though he was looking at someone, something else.

'I am really sorry Rayna. I need to go, it is not you, it is me. You are a really nice person; I am so sorry.' He was almost running now as he grabbed his coat and fled to the door. In front of him was the woman of his dreams disappearing into the dark windswept evening, behind him the woman of his reality, dejected and confused.

The biting cold hit him the second he burst through the pub doors and out into the road. The dim glow of the streetlamps barely lit the dark cars and gloomy buildings. It was starting to rain as the occasional taxi crept past, the headlights reflecting off the surroundings to give everything a ghostly sheen. Robert was in a panic; he had lost her. His eyes darted from one end of the street to the other, not a soul was out on this dank miserable evening. The loneliness outside perfectly matching the mood of the woman he had abandoned inside the pub. And then his eyes caught the faintest of movement in the gloom. The merest hint of human flesh as it disappeared into a side street. *It was her, it had to be. The woman, those legs, it must be her. I have to see her face; I have to know who she is.*

He went hurtling around the corner, *surely, he would catch her now.* It had only been a few seconds since she had gone this way. But in his haste Robert lost his footing, his feet slid from under him in the rain and his body crashed and slid from the pavement into the road.

'Fucking bastard.' Robert pulled himself up in shock. His hands had taken the impact from the fall and blood was oozing out of the scrapes and cuts to his fingers. The new suit was covered in dead leaves and dirty rain. He stood in the middle of the road and laughed, not a laugh of joy but one of pity and shame.

'What the fuck is wrong with me? You stupid fucking big idiot. What in fucks name am I doing chasing some stupid woman that I have never met? For God's sake I have not even seen her face, why am I such an idiot?' He was shouting the words, at the wind, at the rain, at himself.

Certainly not at any other human being, because no one was around to hear, no one was around to care. Robert was about to walk back to the pub, *maybe he could repair the damage he had done with Rayna?* He doubted it though, by now she probably thought he was crazy. He brushed the wet leaves from the front of his suit, water and dirt dripping from his hands.

Number 26, why could he not take his eyes off the gloomy little Terrace house? Robert walked back onto the pavement. The streetlamps and rain adding to the melancholy atmosphere. There were no lights on in the building, there was no logical reason why he felt compelled to knock on the front door. It was the same feeling he had when he stared at the woman, that same feeling of being caught in a trance. It was not that he was being forced against his will towards the house, but he felt as if he was floating to the door. Almost as if the act of moving, placing one foot in front of the other, had nothing to do with him. He reached up to ring the bell. It was so dark the only thing Robert could make out was the white metal numbers pinned underneath the frosted glass of the entrance. His fingers fumbled around the dark frame trying to locate the bell but before he could find it the door had slid open. Even in the dark, he knew it was her. The slender fingers of her warm soft hand guided him into the house.

His eyes followed the silhouette as she slowly climbed the staircase that faced the front door. It was just possible to make her out as the faint glow from the streetlights shone through the glass. He closed the door and silently walked after the woman he so desired. Once she had reached the top of the stairs it was impossible to see her. She had melted into the blackness of the building. And yet, he knew exactly where she was, and where she was leading him to. He heard her hand take hold of the bedroom door and push it open. Inside was pitch black. Robert walked in and the dark shape, now behind him, closed the door.

It was probably only seconds, but it felt so much longer. Even though it was dark, Robert could sense that it was not just the two of them in the room. He did not speak, why would he? She had planned all this; she was in control. He knew that he had to allow things to move towards their natural conclusion. He was the audience in this play, she and whoever else was in the room were the actors. He felt her hand slide into his. Warm, comforting, familiar. And then the light flooded into the room as she pressed the switch with her other hand. Robert should have been shocked at the sight that greeted him, but he wasn't. He understood now, of course, it was obvious. Maybe he had known from the very first time Colin had told him that he needed to, *get back in the marketplace.*

In the large double bed facing him were three women. They wore blindfolds over their eyes and their hands were tightly bound behind their backs. Tape covered their mouths. Robert turned around to finally look at the face of the woman he had waited five long years to see again. Karen, his deceased wife smiled warmly at him. She pulled him closer towards her, their bodies melting into each other. She whispered into his ear, 'You must go now, Robert, my love. I will finish this and then we will be back together. I will never leave you again, I promise.' He understood and started to open the door. He could not help it, his body involuntarily turned back to the three captives struggling on the large bed.

'Lorna, Briony and of course Rayna, I am sorry things never turned out for us. But you must understand, there is only one woman for me. There has only ever been one woman.' He kissed Karen on the lips and walked through the door. Behind him, he could make out the terrified whimpers of the three women. His dead bride bent down to lift the large carving knife into her hand and slowly she floated towards the bed.

(Curtain Call)

Colin edged along the path towards the front of 26 Byron Crescent. He walked slowly, desperately trying to delay the moment when he would have to rattle the door and watch the shambling figure of his brother approach through the glass. Colin looked at the unkempt lawn and thought back to last year. He had been so optimistic about his sibling then. For just a few short months Robert had pulled his life together, at least tried to move forward. The dates had all ended badly. Colin knew it was because Robert, no matter how hard he tried, would end up talking about her. And now it seemed that his brother had completely given up. He seemed more contented but the old clothes and the endless talking about Karen were back with a vengeance. It was as if Robert's wife had never passed away, almost as if her ghost still lived in the house.

Robert slid the door open and turned to walk back towards the kitchen. 'Oh, it is nice to see you too Rob.' Colin said the words with the usual sarcasm he kept for these visits.

'Do you want a cup of bloody tea or not?' Colin followed his brother into the kitchen and gave him a resigned smile. Meanwhile, upstairs in the bedroom, the curtains shuffled slightly to one side. As if they had been moved by the slightest breath of air.

OUR LADY OF THE QUARRY

(Then)

It was Robin who plucked up the courage to go first. Even at the age of seven, he understood the danger he was putting himself in. Kate looked on, a worried frown across her face. If anything happened to her younger brother, she would get the blame. *Mum will kill me if he slips.* She was less than two years older than her sibling and yet every fall and misdemeanour would see the blame laid at her feet. *You are supposed to look after your younger brother, he is only little.* Kate turned around to face the opposite way and then slowly, ever so slowly, she too edged her way down the rock face of the old quarry.

It took them nearly thirty minutes to finally reach terra firma one hundred feet below. Robin was already off running, exploring the secret hidden world they had discovered. Kate scanned the whole area, trying to take in the strange surroundings. The quarry walls spread out all around them. On the far side was a large corrugated iron and stone building. It sloped upwards from the ground back to the surface. Attached to the outside was a rotten wooden staircase. The young girl was already acknowledging that there might be a safer way to escape from the massive manmade hole in the ground. Her eyes finally focused on the centre of the quarry. A large lake had filled up with water, at one time the excavation had gone much deeper.

'Kate, Kate, come and see this. Come and see what I have found.' Her brother's excited chatter brought the young girl back to the present. Without speaking she skipped off after him, running through the puddles and broken discarded stone that littered the ground. The rock wall curved around into a part of the quarry that had been hidden from view. Kate looked at the vision in front of her, startled at first and then she became as animated as her brother. Robin was already climbing into one of the rusting old heaps. Everywhere they looked they could see rotting lorries, disintegrating buses, and even a few moulding cars. Someone older would have quickly realised that there must be an easier way in and out of the quarry. How else could the wrecks have got here, but Kate was already eying up the old staircase as their way to escape.

Robin sat in the driver's seat of an old single deck bus. He pretended to turn the heavy steering wheel while making engine noises as he threading his way down the imaginary highway. Kate scrambled over broken glass and twisted metal to join him. Scattered along the passenger deck of the bus she could see wet pages of a long-discarded soft porn magazine. Immediately the instinct an older sister has to protect her sibling kicked in. 'Robin, wow look at that truck over in the corner. Let's collect the stones and drive them to the building site.' Her descriptive game was enough to distract her younger brother who bounced out of the side door of the bus without noticing the naked ladies laying crumpled in the pools of dirty water. Kate was already beginning to regret the time and energy they had expended climbing down into the quarry. She knew how dangerous this place could be and was afraid that someone might see them. *Mum will kill me if the police take us back to our house.* The discovery of the old vehicles was bad news. Kate had hoped that Robin would quickly tire of wandering around the quarry floor, but now that he had found this children's playground of rusting hulks, it would be difficult to get him to leave.

Kate stepped out of the bus, her eyes were drawn to the myriad little puddles scattered between the heaps of broken rock and old wrecks. She walked over to the nearest one and peered down. The Spring sun reflected off the shimmering water causing her eyes to hurt. It took a few seconds for the young girl's vision to focus. At her feet, she could see hundreds of tiny specs weaving from side to side in the pool. This was her chance to distract her brother and get him away from the scrap graveyard. She turned and shouted, 'Robin, Robin, come and see the frogs spawn, there are thousands of them, thousands. Robin, Robin.' Kate could feel a slight panic rising in her body, the truck she expected to see him sitting in was empty. It took a full five minutes of wandering through the maze of ancient rust before she finally spied her brother. He was sitting in an old car that no longer held any glass in its windows. The back seat was missing, and the branches of a young sapling protruded from the absent rear bonnet.

'Kate, I found a Rolls Royce. I am going to drive up the side of the quarry and take us home. Come on, get in or you will be left behind.' She laughed and climbed into the filthy seat beside him. Even she knew that this had not been a

Rolls Royce when it was alive.

'Robin, we need to try and find a way out of here. Mum will be expecting us home for tea at five. I don't know what the time is, but we have to go now.'

'No, no I am going to drive us home Kate, in this car. I need to get petrol and then we can go.' Kate sighed and tried a different approach.

'Robin, I found thousands of frogs in the puddles, you have to come and see them. They are giants.' The statement did the trick. He turned around to face her with his eyes wide in anticipation.

'Ok, yes, let's go and see the frogs but what shall we do about her?' Kate stared at him, a look of confusion causing the young girl to frown. *What on earth was he on about now?*

'Do about who Robin?' Her brother pointed to the car about ten yards away, facing directly towards them. At one time it had probably been black but now just a few flecks of paint hung on in a sea of orange rust. It had lain on the bed of the quarry for so long that its wheels had disappeared into the dirt. The struts holding the roof had rotted causing it to lay at a precarious angle, almost ready to collapse onto the seats below.

'What shall we say to her?' Kate's eyes finally saw what

he was pointing at. Sitting looking at them from the wreck was the figure of a young woman. She stared back at them, her body taught and motionless. Her white face half-covered by straggling black curls. She was as pale as death, but they knew she was real. She was watching their every move.

(Now)

It had been a long time since I had seen her. So many years since we had spoken. How can a brother and sister once so close become strangers? Of course, she was in my thoughts, but life takes over and gradually that separation becomes a chasm. You see the person you once loved disappearing farther and farther into the distance until their shape, their voice, their memory is placed in storage. Filed away in the library of time to gather dust.

It was not just Kate that I wanted to see again, it was the quarry. Does that seem strange to you? I did not understand it either and yet I had to go back. It was more than fifty years since I had last scaled that rock face and walked amongst the mechanical dead. We had only visited the place twice and yet it held such vivid memories in my heart. I know why but it was only now, in the last years of my life that I could admit it. The day I walked away from the quarry, the black lake, the tadpoles, and the rotting metal, that was the last time I was really happy. Nothing was ever the same again.

I suppose it was our mother passing away last year that prompted me to make the re-connection. Kate had always seemed to be afraid of her. I think she thought of me as being the favourite and maybe she had a point. Does being the older sibling, even if it is just a few years, burden you with the responsibility of taking care of the younger child? After the funeral, I spent long hours looking at Google earth and scouring over old maps. The quarry is no longer there, it has long been filled in. Nowadays the thought of a massive unprotected hole full of water and old cars seems ridiculous. But this was the norm in the sixties. Once they had finished with something, quarries, buildings, railway lines, they simply left them to rot. No fences, no signs, just a magnet for children to play in. According to what I read on the internet, it had been filled in during the late seventies and was now a nature reserve. This gave me some hope that there might be something to find, something that would allow me to understand what it was all about.

I wanted to take my time, devour each second before I set foot in Belfast again. The memory seemed to become clearer each year, the further it went away in time the closer it felt. I stepped onto the ferry at Cairnryan just outside Stranraer. I could have flown; my wife could not understand why I would want to make a tedious train journey from Glasgow and a ferry crossing. Was I frightened of what I might find? Was I worried about the reception I might receive? I probably was, I knew I had left it far too long. It was guilt.

(Then)

The two children eyed each other over the small dining table. The boy's face spoke of secrets and excitement, the girl's was more of anticipation and concern. 'Kate, make sure you are back by eight o'clock. Put the oven on at eight-fifteen. I have set it to the right temperature. Don't forget now will you.'

'Yes, mum. Eight-fifteen, put the oven on.' Kate watched attentively as her mother placed the coat around her shoulders and hurried to the door.

'Tell your father that I will be back at nine. It is an early finish at the bakery today with-it being Friday. Kate, look after your brother and if you are going out to play, stay away from trouble.' The words were spoken on autopilot, the mother knew the children were not taking them in.

'Yes mum, and yes I will put the oven on at eight-fifteen to heat dad's dinner for him.' The older woman was just about to open the back door of the house and leave when she stopped and turned back to look at Kate. She said nothing for a few seconds as though she was lost in thought. The young girl stared back at her mother, their eyes meeting.

'Kate. You know I love you, don't you?' Her daughter looked away and did not reply. The older woman finally turned to head out of the door, her usual stern aura quickly returning.

'Don't forget your dad's tea in the oven. I shall see you both later.'

Robin was running as fast as his short legs would allow. Kate followed close behind. It had been almost a week since their first visit to the quarry. The long days at school had dragged on as each child waited in anticipation for the weekend to start. They had originally planned to go tomorrow as Saturday would give them more time. Robin could not wait until then. He insisted they visit it that Friday evening once their mother had gone off to do her shift at the bakery. No amount of pleading from Kate would make him change his mind. And yet, even though she knew it was a risk going this late, she too wanted to go back and see if they could find the pale lady.

'Robin, promise me you will leave when I tell you. We have to be back to put dad's dinner on. It will be dangerous if we are still in the quarry when it gets dark.

'Yes, yes, promise, cross my heart and hope to die.' Robin was running down the little alleyway separating the derelict cottages that backed onto the quarry. Kate could see that he had his fingers crossed behind his back. She had long ago accepted that her little brother would say one thing and do the opposite.

'No, Robin. We are not climbing down; it is too dangerous. Let's go around to the hole in the gate at the entrance.' But her brother as always ignored his sisters pleading and was already scrambling over the edge of the rockface. Kate peered into the hundred-foot drop with a worried frown. She watched her brother slide slowly down towards the black lake and then turned to make the descent after him.

'Do you think she will be there Robin?' Her brother answered from a few feet below.

'Who?'

'Our lady of the Quarry. The ghost lady.'

'You can't call her, our lady of the quarry, that's against the law.' Kate edged down a few feet further, trying to keep up with her brother.

'What are you talking about Robin? Why can't I call her that?'

'Because our lady is God's wife. My teacher told me, and the priest said it as well.' Kate tried to keep up with both her rapidly descending sibling's agility as well as his reasoning.

'No Robin don't talk daft. God does not have a wife. You are thinking about Mary, she was Jesus's mum.' The only sound Kate could hear for the next few moments was Robin panting as his feet and hands looked for holds on the dusty rockface. Like all boys, he had to be right and she knew he would be thinking up a reply.

'I am not daft. Our lady is God's wife, it says so in the holy bible, so there Miss Stinky pants.' Kate laughed and continued to scramble downwards after her little brother.

It took them nearly an hour to find the car they had seen the woman in but now it sat empty. The light wind whistled around the multitude of decaying trucks and buses surrounding the smaller wrecks. Kate felt both disappointed and relieved. She had hoped to see the strange figure again, but she was also wise enough to know that the apparition could be a bad omen. The young girl did not doubt that the pale lady was a ghost. No living person would sit so still and silent. No mortal soul would wait amongst the rusting dead unless they too had left this earth.

Robin had already lost interest in the woman, ghost or not. He darted in and out of each and every one of the archaic statues to a long-faded motoring age. Searching for the next buzz, the next hit that every seven-year-old seems to crave. Kate walked over to the edge of the black lake and peered into the filthy murky water. The edges of the bank slid sharply down and then disappeared into the forgotten depths. She picked up a loose piece of rock and dropped it in. It made a deep splashing sound and then slid from view. The ripples on the water spread out from where the stone had sunk. They moved out in a uniform pattern towards each side of the black lake. As her eyes followed them, she could make out the reflection of the old wooden staircase attached to the side of the disused quarry building in the distance. Instinctively she looked up and saw the woman standing at the top of the stairs, motionless but always pale, always looking. It was only then that it dawned on Kate that the pale lady was not watching them, it was watching her.

Kate instinctively started to walk around the black lake in an attempt to get closer. She finally stopped at the corner within a few feet of the water and waved. The pale lady did not respond, she continued to stare as if she was boring a hole into the young girl's soul.

'Kate, Kate, look, quick look.' The shriek of Robin's voice shocked Kate out of her trance. She swayed slightly forward and for a second her body tensed at the thought that she might slip into the dark water. Kate turned and ran towards the sound of her brother's voice. It was coming from the bus, the one they had investigated when they first discovered the scrap yard. He was kneeling, holding a piece of dirty dripping paper in his little fingers.

'Kate, look. This lady has got booby things. Why has she not got her clothes on?' He was chuckling and pointing at the soggy picture.

'Wow, what is that. Kate, she has not got a dingle. Has it fallen off?' His sister sighed before answering.

'She is a girl; they don't have dingles, Robin. Only men have dingles.' The boy looked at her with a childish grin across his face.

'That's rubbish. If girls don't have dingles, then how do they do a pee?'

In the panic of hearing her brother shout, Kate had forgotten about the pale lady. She bent down and looked through one of the broken glass windows of the bus. The apparition had gone but that was not what startled her. The sun had fallen below the rockface walls that surrounded the quarry. Suddenly it had become gloomy. It was still easy enough to see but Kate knew that time was getting on.

'We need to go, Robin. Put that down, we need to go. Dad will be home before us, and mum will go nuts if we do not have his dinner on in the oven.' Rather than listen to his protests she grabbed her sibling and marched him to the door. He could sense the fear in her voice and for once did as she asked him. The two children started to run around the edge of the black lake. A winding gravel road led up to a locked gate at the top of the quarry. They had used it the last time they visited after making an initial attempt to climb the wooden staircase. It had been so rotten that after a few steps Kate had put her foot through one of the moulding stair planks.

Just before the start of the drive, the gap between the quarry wall and the pool became only three or four feet. Kate was leading, now in a panic at the thought that she might get into trouble from her mum. Robin was falling behind.

'Wait for me you big stinky. It's not fair, you are running too fast.'

Suddenly his foot caught the edge of the bank and he was sliding down, slipping towards the deep black water. Robin tried desperately to grab hold of something to arrest his fall, but all his hands could find was the loose rock. Slowly, his body slid towards the water-filled chasm. His feet had now reached the edge of the cold lake and he could feel its icy grip reaching out to drag him into the hidden depths. The young boy was terrified, he knew he was sliding to certain death and he was screaming in terror.

'Kate, Kate, help, help...Kate.'

His body was now half-submerged as he edged down inch by inch. He tried to stop wriggling to see if it would slow his descent but still, the black mass pulled him further and further in. It was oozing over his body now, his screams growing sharper and more desperate.

'Kate, I am going to drown, Kate, Kate...'

Now the water curled up around his neck and the first shards of the filthy liquid started to float towards his mouth and trickle into his lungs. And then the blackness came and surrounded his tiny body, silent and dark. She was in the water with him, a dreamlike shadow smiling, holding out her white hands towards the little boy. The pale lady pulling and pushing him towards the surface. Her black curls flowing around her face. Her mouth open to accept in the putrid contents of the lake. He was floating, gliding from side to side like the minuscule tadpoles as they skated over the mouldy picture of the naked woman. Merging with the rusting hulks and forgotten possessions of the long dead.

(Now)

I parked the car in front of one of the little bungalows. In the sixties this had been a new estate, now it looked tired. In the intervening years, the surrounding countryside had been eaten up. The houses were now part of Belfast city rather than on the periphery. It felt intrusive to be here, I no longer belonged. Maybe I never did. Kate did not want me to come back. I could feel her words rattling in my head, *you need to forget, you cannot live in the past forever.*

I was not sure if I was even looking at the right house. It seemed to be the one we had lived in, the number on the door confirmed it. Despite having been rebuilt with a loft extension as well as added ground floor rooms, it seemed small. Maybe as a seven-year-old everything in your past remains large. I still have a photograph of me looking out of my bedroom window. My mum must have taken it on my seventh birthday in 1967. I am holding a toy yellow crane with a smile spread across my face. A real happy smile, not a forced photograph one. I know why, it was the crane. I had not expected this additional present. It had chains and little gears. As you turned each of the tiny levers, the mechanical digger arm would move and scoop up the earth. Now in my sixties when I look at the picture, it is not the toy crane that makes me smile. It is Kate, she has accidentally invaded the photograph and you can see half of her face. She too is smiling, even though no doubt my mum was telling her off for ruining the picture. Money was tight in those days and one photograph a year, usually on your birthday, was the norm.

I left the estate feeling empty, it had not stirred my emotions the way I had hoped it would. I suppose I only went to see the old house so that I would not feel guilty about searching for the quarry. I had no memory of how to find our childhood playground. My knowledge came from studying old maps on my computer back home. I had the route planned out; it would take me to the nature reserve. It had to be the place, nothing else looked right. My heart was pumping as I crossed the busy main dual carriageway and headed towards what looked like some rundown industrial buildings. They were fenced off, but a modern green sign pointed towards a gap that led to the area I wanted to explore.

There could be little doubt that I was standing at the very point of my childhood dreams as well as my adult nightmares. The stony ground edged up to the border of the nature reserve before turning into soft grass alive with trees and bracken. Little paths twisted and turned through the marshy ground, disappearing around corners to be swallowed up by the flowing greenery. I did not need to take another step. In my mind, it was still a one-hundred-foot drop, down to the rusting graves of the mechanical dead and the deep black water. When we were children Kate had implored me not to climb down to the quarry. Even now she was asking me not to go back.

Do not go down, do not take one more step. The pale woman will be waiting. Tell her goodbye, let this be the end. I love you, my little brother. Let her go.

For the first time in my life, I voluntarily did as my older sister asked and turned to go back to my car.

(Then)

The headmaster stood up to face the throng of silent children. For once the gathered mass of little people did not need to be told to settle down and be quiet. Even at that age, the young can recognise death and give it the respect it deserves. Well, maybe that is not entirely true. If you tell a child that their auntie they rarely see or hardly knew has passed away, they pretend to care so as not to offend. In reality, they are already thinking about the next game, the friends they want to see, the adult rules they can break. We all do it, don't consider yourself as a bad person. Childhood is the only time you get to be wrapped up in yourself. Surrounded by your own adventure and no one else matters. No, it is only when you tell a youngster that one of their own, another child has died, then they go silent and listen. At that age, it seems impossible to die. It comes as a shock to all when one of the little people falls.

Children, I know you will all join me in prayer. Prayer for one of our loved and respected pupils who was found dead last week. Let this be a warning to you all. The Ballina quarry is strictly out of bounds. It is an extremely dangerous place and any child found entering it will be in serious trouble. Sadly, we lost a beloved classmate who along with her brother was tempted to break into private property. Kate Patterson will be remembered as the wise smiling little girl who was always looking after her little brother Robin Patterson. And yet in death comes life. Kate drowned while making a successful rescue attempt after her little brother fell into the quarry lake. This was an entirely unselfish act as Kate in knowing she could hardly swim, still saved Robin from certain death. We wish our fellow pupil Robin Patterson a swift recovery in Belfast Royal Hospital. We also give remembrance and prayers to Kate Patterson. Let her death be a warning to all of you but let us not forget the bravery she showed in life.

Kate Patterson, Born June 1958, died April 1967.

(Now)

Why had it taken me 52 years to forgive? Only now could I accept that it was not Kate's fault, or mine or our mother's. Someone has to be unlucky; someone has to be the victim. The ripples on the water spread out and that one stone, that one splash impacts us all for the rest of our lives. It is a sad thing to say but maybe the one who dies so young is really the shining light. The eternal child who burns forever brightly. They never have to grow old and become admired, hated, loved, an enemy, a soul mate, an adult. The pale lady and the child, forever floating in the dark water like a shimmering memory to lost youth.

Car Graveyard

Metallic, shiny, once loved

King of the B road, once someone's pride, once someone's joy

Rusted, grass-grown, lonely except for its silent decaying friends.

No piston roar, no ignition spark, just memories of happy miles tread

Metal, rubber, glass, once polished, once caressed

King of the A road, once someone's friend, once someone's desire

Broken, going, merging back into the earth

No piston roar, no ignition spark

Just a mirror of time, just a bearer of life.

SUMMER (RUSTY PETROL PUMPS)

I think you can pinpoint the happiest time in your life by the age you are at that moment. Look, I completely understand that circumstances will be very different for each individual but stick with my logic for a few seconds on this if you don't mind.

I was at my most contented around the age of four, it might even have been three, but it is hard to remember back more than fifty years. You see, and here comes the theory bit, being four must be a perfect age. You are old enough to be aware of your surroundings and if you are lucky enough, you live in a perfect little protected bubble. You could say that being one or two is the same but who remembers being that old? No, it has to be four, maybe three but probably four. It is that age when you can do whatever you want, and it comes just before life ruins everything by throwing school and other kids in your way.

Ok, so you are probably thinking, how about proving your point with some examples. Maybe you are not thinking that at all, maybe you are thinking, I was happiest at eight, or thirty-two because that was when you won the lottery or met the love of your life. Well, it is my story so for continuity, would you mind if we stick with four being top dog, just for now. Eight was crap for me anyway and if I am being honest thirty-two was pretty shite as well.

I was four in the early sixties, well 1964, I suppose that is early to mid-sixties. We lived in a cardboard cut-out, lost little English village called Norton. Near the town of Daventry in Northamptonshire. It was that last period before modern Britain infiltrated Edwardian England. Most of the inhabitants of the village had been born there. It still had a blacksmith (seriously, no kidding) and a real village pub selling beer. Eating in pubs had yet to be invented. The one little shop supplied everything you needed until the weekly visit to the big town of Daventry. It had a church that seemed massive to me but, well more of that later. And wait for it, do you know what else it had? It had a garage, one that fixed your car and even sold petrol. One of those garages you see on old postcards. Rusty petrol pumps, bits of engine everywhere and the smell of oil permeating the rustic stone building.

My mother used to walk the 2.5 miles to Daventry with me chattering contentedly by her side. Lorry drivers would stop and offer us a lift, mum was only in her early twenties and rather naive. We would jump up into the cab and despite the driver probably having ulterior motives, we survived without being found strangled in a nearby field. On the days when no lift was offered, we would arrive at the railway bridge on the edge of the town. I loved that bridge; it meant the long slog was over. You have to realise that I was a small four-year-old, I am not much taller now. I always hoped to see a train crossing the bridge. Why do kids love trains? I never did but my mum would always lie to me and say, it goes to the sugar factory, next time we will see a train for sure. When I think back, it always seemed to be bright and sunny. Does the memory of being happy automatically insert the sun into any recollection?

My sister was eighteen months older than me. I think that must be why most of my memories before school age do not have her in them. She would have already been at the children's prison a year or two before me. I remember one lovely sunny day (Here we go again), I and my sister were out walking down a country lane. I spotted one of those old-fashioned haystacks in a field and asked her what it was. She told me it was a farmer's toy shop and if we collected enough wildflowers then we could choose what toy we wanted. Toys were something you only received at Christmas, so I worked like a Trojan for the next few days collecting flowers. I kept asking my sister when we would be going to exchange them for free toys but by then she had moved onto her next scam.

I can't place my father in my memories of that time, but I know I had one. He would constantly moan at me when I became a teenager so he must have existed before then. My dad worked for the BBC; I think he climbed those massive transmitter masts. Don't ask me why, maybe he liked heights. My mother used to go potato picking with all the other village women. It was back-breaking work, but we needed the money. Even at that age, I was expected to muck in although, like most men, I tried everything to skive and let the women do the work. They would often find old Roman coins and other artefacts. There was a story that someone discovered the decomposed body of a complete Roman Warrior in a field next to where we toiled. I must have been a cynical bastard even at the age of four. I remember saying to my mum, *that sounds like a right load of old crap*. Or words to that effect anyway.

My sister's friends seemed to like me. They thought I was cute, and I would be allowed to join in their games. Making dens in the woods and chasing each other through the green fields. Being four is perfect for chatting up the girls. They would have only been a few years older than me, but they seemed so tall and clever. That was my peak at being comfortable with women, it was never as easy as that again.

I started at primary school in Daventry when I was four and a half. I love the way kids talk in halves about their age. Imagine standing in the pub with a big bunch of burly men and telling them you were fifty-nine and a half. I and my sister would get the bus from our village to Daventry in the morning and then back at night. In my first week, I left my school bag on the bus. When I got home and my mum found out, she borrowed a neighbours bike and cycled to the police station in Daventry. The Sergeant in the little office telephoned the bus garage and having found my bag, they promised to drop it off at the station. That evening a police car turned up at our little house and handed over my school bag. Innocent times indeed. No one had any money, phones or even a television but somehow the sun always shone. I still lose things even now. You have more chance of being tasered by a tiny Policewoman dressed in armour these days than getting your school bag handed back by them.

The first shadow to invade my perfect little world came when my mother mentioned to my dad about a suicide on the railway line. The mainline to London passed a mile or so away from the village. A young mother had committed suicide by jumping in front of a train with her child. That was the first time I had even heard of death and from then on, the dark clouds of life started to gather in the distance. They became a storm just a few months later when our little innocent English village family moved to Belfast. Catholics and especially English ones were not welcome in a country that was about to explode. Within a day of arriving there, I heard the word fuck being used. From that point on, it became a fight for survival.

It would have been the early 1990's before I set foot in Norton again. Those childhood years had been such a happy time that I did not want to go back and ruin the memory. I am a nosey bugger though so of course I did. The village looked just like I remembered it. The little wall my mother built using old rocks still stood at the front of our house. The building looked so much smaller than I remembered, which is strange because the church now looked enormous. The garage was long gone, and the pub was now one of those places that had menus and sold food. I drove on to Daventry, along that same winding road my mother's ghost still walked. The railway bridge was gone, obliterated by a large busy roundabout. It was only then that I accepted I would never see the train going into the sugar factory, despite my mother's promises. I forgive her though, and my sister for making me collect wildflowers for two days.

LADY CROWTHORN'S CHRISTMAS PRESENT

Here he comes. I would like to say right on cue but nothing Lord Crowthorn has ever done could be described as on cue. His wife Lady Elizabeth Crowthorn would berate him during the early years of their marriage but now, let us just say, she had given up. It was not that he was a deliberately difficult man, more the fact that with money and little responsibility he could do what we all would love to do. Lord Fenston Crowthorn simply pleased himself, all day and every day. That is why we are standing at the top of Flender's field watching this jovial drunk stagger up the little country road to Elphinstone House, the home of the Crowthorn's since the clock first ticked.

Lady Elizabeth was out in the garden, taking advantage of the unusually bright weather for early November. Beside her stood the small stooped figure of Brendon Speckler, the head gardener. Well, I use the title head gardener in the loosest terms. He was the only gardener at this time of year. Come the summer he might be joined by a few of the local village boys to help him. For the Crowthorn's money was tight but the old titles remained. So, they still had a housekeeper, a butler and a head gardener who in theory looked after the ground staff at Elphinstone House but in reality, the ground staff was him. Oh, of course. I nearly forgot young Rosie Thresher, the local village girl. She helped in the kitchen. She helped in other places as well but more of that later. One last point before you start to feel sorry for Lord and Lady Crowthorn, money might have been tight but trust me. They still had a darn site more cash than me and you. Well me at least, maybe you won the lottery? Well done if you did, respect. Any chance of a loan of a tenner until I get paid on Friday?

Lady Elizabeth sighed as she looked at the empty flower beds filled with dead leaves. 'Mr. Speckler, I think next year we need to up our game somewhat regarding summer colour.'

'Yes, sommer color Lady Lizbeth, sommer color.' Brendon said the words with no emotion at all.

'I mean it really would be frightfully lovely to work a plan next year. Get planting early Mr. Speckler. We shall think ahead this time; I shall help you. We really could make this a floral delight, a rampant splash of vivid colour.'

'Yes, lots of vivid color, lots of vivid color Lady Lizbeth.' Old Brendon Speckler would be lucky to keep on top of cutting the massive lawns next year, never mind splashing vivid colour around the flower beds. They had this conversation every year and both knew it was just idle talk. Having given her annual horticulture lecture to the gardener Lady Crowthorn turned dismissively and walked back to the large front door of Elphinstone House. The old gardener sighed and continued without enthusiasm to sweep the winter leaves from the lawn.

It was not long before he heard a voice approaching from the winding drive. He muttered quietly to himself making sure not to be heard. 'Aw fer fuck sake, here comes that other fucking idiot now.' The other fucking idiot he was referring to was Lord Crowthorn who was staggering haphazardly towards him.

'Ahh Speckler, Mr. Speckler, the world's greatest gardener bar none.' Old Brendon knew that any drunken compliment from his Lordship usually meant he was looking for a favour.

'Be wanting something then M'Lord?' Fenston moved his face within a few inches of the gardener. The old man attempted to back away without being rude, but his master had lost the ability to be aware of keeping to his own personal space. The Black Oak in the village only opened between 11 and 2 on a weekday and yet his Lordship had still managed to down his regular six pints and four whiskys. He called it his morning taster, *gets me oiled up and ready for the real opening time at 6 p.m.*

'Yes, I was Speckler, I was indeedy the doody. I was wondering, have you seen the lady of the house about Speck the Speckler?'

'Be just seen er not two minutes ago sur. She wur tellin me bout next year's plants she wur.'

'Ahh right, right. I was hoping she might have gone to Bicester, done a bit of shopping.' Fenston winked at the gardener. He knew what was coming next from his tipsy employer. 'I don't suppose you have seen Rosie about have you Speck the Speckler?'

'Be Rosie day arf Sur. You be forgotten it be Wednesday, turday Sur.'

'Of Feck, of course. Bloody Wednesdays. Oh well,

Mr. Specko Specsteroony. Enjoy your work, whatever it is you are doing.' And with that, the drunk Lord Fenston Crowthorn staggered off towards the large mansion. The Gardener shook his head and laughed. He liked his Lordship, even more so when he was drunk. That meant he liked him all the time as Fenston was permanently pickled. He was not that keen on Lady Elizabeth though, but that was just because she gave him work to do.

As Fenston stumbled through the main door of Elphinstone House, his foot caught on the hallway carpet and he was sent crashing to the ground. His long-suffering wife heard the commotion and walked calmly from the reception room; she knew it would be him. She looked down at her errant husband who by now had rolled onto his back and was staring up at her.

'Lizzy, I feel age is catching up on me my dear. This is the second time this week I have tripped in the house. I must have Alzheimer's or maybe a touch of winter flu coming on. What say you, old girl?'

'Don't old girl me, Fenston Crowthorn. The only reason you trip over is that you are permanently pickled.' She said the words without malice. Elizabeth had long ago given up on trying to change her husband. He had been drunk for so long she could not remember what he was like sober. In the early days of their marriage, she had been embarrassed by his antics but after so many years she had simply become immune. And, at least he was a happy drunk. I suppose you would consider Fenston to be a functioning alcoholic, barely functioning but functioning none the less. Anyway, he had nothing to function over. Lord Crowthorn was used to everyone else doing the work.

'Sorry old girl, I mean Lizzy, I mean Elizabeth. Did I tell you that you look simply stunning today my darling?' He pulled himself up from the floor and stood shakily in front of her. His wife smiled wearily back at him.

'Oh Fenston, please do not give me that old tosh. Save the words for the chambermaid Rosie, the one you are always chatting up.' Fenston took a step back in mock indignation and nearly fell over his own feet.

'Lizzy, my dearest love, I have no idea what you mean.' Elizabeth had already turned and was walking back to the room she had just come from. Just before disappearing through the door she stopped, as though she had forgotten something and then looked back at him.

'Fenston, you know I don't mind what you get up to. But you know sometimes, well…'

'What is it dearest, sweetest lady in all Europe including the outer reaches of the Amazon forest?' For once Fenston was listening. Elizabeth never told him off or complained about anything. This was unusual.

'Oh, it is nothing, just forget it Fenston. Anyway, you had better get your afternoon nap in or you might sleep through six o'clock opening time at the Black Oak.' Her husband refused to let the matter drop; she had piqued his drunken interest now.

'My dear, my darling, my sweetest lady in all of Africa. Do tell me, what is it that bothers you?'

'Well, it is just, just. Well, you never remember anything. I mean important dates, like our anniversary or, well just anything. I mean when was the last time you bought me a present?'

'My darling, my lady of the forest, my scented spring candle. How can you say such a thing? I may not buy you presents but I do remember. It is just that I assume you know I love you more than the stars in the sky, more than the water in the ocean, more th…'

'Well, what is today then Fenston?' This question shook him a little. She was on the attack now and he was cornered. For once his rambling charm was falling on deaf ears.

'Today, you say today. Why, today is Tuesday. What yes, it is Tuesday my peach plucked straight from the tree of God.'

'Fenston, it is Wednesday, not Tuesday. That is not the question I am asking. I mean why is today special?' It suddenly dawned on Lord Crowthorn that his wife had already given him the answer and it had passed over him. The lightbulb in his head suddenly switched on and he grasped the opportunity to get out of the hole he was digging.

'Of course, I know what day it is my petal, my rose in bloom. It is our anniversary of course. And we have been married for, well for a long time my beautiful.' Elizabeth stared at him for a few seconds longer before shaking her head and turning to walk away. She was almost out of earshot but Lord Crowthorn could just about make out her final words.

'It is my birthday today, my 70th birthday. Maybe, just maybe sometimes, it would be nice to get a present, Fenston.'

It was only ten minutes after six o'clock opening time and yet the usual village booze bags had already assembled in the Black Oak. Some of them would have waited at the door for Geoff Stannerwix the Landlord to open the pub. They would hear the various locks being unbolted and sigh with contentment at the thought of their first beer. This contrasted with the disappointment they all felt only four hours previously on hearing the dreaded words, *Time Gentlemen Please.*

It is common knowledge that every pub has one person, usually an old man who sits propped up on the same seat at the bar every day. The Black Oak was no exception to this rule, in fact, it could boast six permanent drunks. They were lined up in the usual order on the tall stools at the bar. This Wednesday evening, we had, Tony the Taxi, so-called because he used to drive a cab. That was a long time ago though, in fact so long ago no one could ever recall him actually driving a taxi. Beside him sat Glib Paddering a part-time salesman. He sold life insurance, but it was hard to imagine the part-time bit as he was full time in the pub. Glib was already asking if anyone wanted a drink as he ordered his second pint, a full ten minutes into opening time. Next came Rufus O'Callaghan. He liked to think he was some sort of mystic Irishman, but he spoke with a soft English accent. He was a big man, rough-looking and yet oddly, he had been an accountant. Retired now of course, as were all the gang at the bar. Rufus was well known for being mean. When it came to his round, he always had an excuse. *I forgot my wallet lads, the bank was shut, if you get another one in, I will get the next two,* and so on. No wonder he had been an accountant, he enjoyed working with other people's money. The last two in the line were the Glander brothers or the twins as most called them. Why they were considered twins, I have no idea. Robbie Glander was short and completely bald while his brother Tobie-Clusterball Glander was tall and some might have said handsome but in an old man sort of way. They had once run a farm together but had been evicted when foot and mouth disease destroyed their dairy business. Well that was what they would like people to believe but many felt it was because the short Glander twin liked to drink and the big Glander twin liked the women. He liked to drink as well if I am being brutally honest.

Usually, by now the group would have been laughing and chatting, but something had upset their routine and most either said nothing and stared at the door or whispered to each other. Even the Landlord Mr. Stannerwix was looking towards the entrance while he wiped the inside of a beer glass with an old stained tea towel.

'He must be dead, has to be. This has never happened

before.' The words from Rufus O'Callaghan could have been taken as genuine concern for the missing Lord Crowthorn but most knew it was because it was his turn at the bar. Fenston was always generous with his money and often covered for the mean accountant who rarely bought a round.

'Maybe I should phone Elphinstone House, his wife Elizabeth might be giving him the kiss of life right at this moment.' A few chuckles followed the comment from Geoff the Landlord as he poured Glib Paddering another pint of beer.

'More likely to be that hot little Rosie, the housemaid who is giving him the kiss of life.' Again, more chuckles as Tony the Taxi joined in the banter.

'If It wur Rosie what gived him the kiss of life then he probably had a heart attack, she could eat him alive.' Tobie Clusterball Glander listened to the words from his brother Robbie with a hint of envy. He had his eye on Rosie, well he had his eye on every woman in the village.

It was at that very moment that the door opened and in walked the errant Lord Crowthorn. Something was wrong because he seemed deep in thought while most would have been expecting him to be panting with desperation for a drink. After all, it was now 6:15. A full quarter of an hour of boozing had been lost, never to be regained. Fenston ignored the jokes directed at him for being late and took his usual position at the bar between Rufus and Taxi. Very soon he was caught up in the usual pub talk. Conversations that go around in circles, sometimes getting heated before ending up in drunken embraces. One-minute sounding like a fistfight might erupt, followed by laughter as they quickly forgot what the subject of the argument was. The Black oak was no different than any other village pub at 6:15 pm. Mostly men, mostly older men I should say, talking nonsense while loving every second of it. An escape from reality for a few hours. Or as in the case of Lord Crowthorn and his buddies, a permanent escape from life.

It was Taxi who noticed that Fenston was not himself. It was just a subtle change but when you drink side by side with someone for so many years, well you get to know them. Crowthorn was still enjoying himself, buying drinks and throwing in comments as required but he seemed slightly distant.

'Something bothering you, Feni? you don't seem yourself. You never really explained why you were so late either.' Taxi whispered the words so the others could not hear. He need not have worried as a heated discussion was going on regarding the average size of the male member. Rufus claimed it was seven inches while others argued that it was far less than that. Most knew that the accountant was only saying that because he wanted to give the impression, he was well endowed. The conversation turned back to woman and cricket after Tobi Cluster-Ball Glander claimed his was a foot long even when it was asleep. The raucous laughter and chatter gave enough cover for Fenston and Taxi to continue their conversation.

'Yes Taxi, I will admit to being slightly perturbed about something. It is a darned business, an absolute dashing cad of a business if I am honest.' Lord Crowthorn lifted his whisky tumbler and poured it into his beer glass before taking a thoughtful swig of the potent mixture.

'Well, I know how you must feel Feni, I used to drive Taxis and I had to handle some tricky situations as well.' The words from Tony caused Lord Crowthorn to look up.

'Did you, did you really by gosh?'

'Yes, yes, I had to deal with some rum situations I can tell you.'

'No, no, I mean did you drive a taxi?' The subtlety of the comment from Fenston was not lost on Tony. He quickly changed the conversation back to the Lord's predicament.

'So, what is it that concerns you then Feni old boy? Did Elizabeth catch you in the arms of that little Rosie?' Lord Crowthorn did not laugh. He still seemed troubled, this was serious, and Tony realised that it might be appropriate to stop making jokes and listen for once.

'It is a rum old affair Taxi. She has thrown me a googly old chap. A rock-solid bouncer of a googly. The old lady has shocked me to the core. I just never expected it of her, a real bounder of a googly, an absolute stonker.'

'What do you mean? Are you talking about your old lady, Elizabeth? Jesus Feni, what has happened? Has she run off with the gardener?'

'Worse, worse than that. Far worse Taxi. A real googly of a ball. Just not cricket, and from Elizabeth of all people.' As he took another sorrowful sip from his beer Lord Crowthorn suddenly became aware of the silence that now surrounded him in the pub. The rest of the drinkers, including the Landlord Geoff Stannerwix, had stopped talking. They all wanted to listen to the outcome of this terrible googly that Elizabeth had bowled at her poor forlorn husband. Even Glib Paddering had let go of his beer glass, this was getting serious. Robbie Glander leaned his little bald pate around the large frame of Rufus O'Callaghan and said the words they all wanted to repeat.

'What the fuck did she do Feni? For fuck sake, spit it out, man? The tension is making me feel sober.' Lord Fenston pulled his body up from the stooped position and sat up straight. It was as if he was trying to summon up the courage to tell them what horror had befallen him at the hands of the Lady of Elphinstone House.

'She told me that I have never bought her a present.'

Would you mind joining me at the top of Flender's field again, just for a moment? I know it is early December and bloody freezing but please humour me just this one last time. Here he comes, look you can see him just beyond that far hedgerow. If you look carefully, maybe use the binoculars, you will notice he has a spring in his step again. Now the reason I mention this is because if you had been around for the last four weeks you too would have been concerned for our boozy Lord Crowthorn. Ever since the shock of being told that he had never purchased a gift for Lady Crowthorn, he had been a troubled man. You could see it in the way he walked. A lost soul with the weight of the world on his shoulders. Not today though, no not today.

The afternoon sun was already dipping below the edge of the earth when Rosie Thresher left through the back door of Elphinstone House. She was glad her shift was over, not that she did much but just the thought of cleaning the endless rooms in the large building was enough to tire her out. Just as she reached the long gravel road that twisted down from the mansion of Elphinstone, she noticed Fenston wandering up the road. He was clearly drunk; well he was always clearly drunk but this time he had added a happy little left/right dance to each step. Rosie spied an opportunity. She liked old Crowthorn, he made her laugh, but business was business.

'I say, Rosie old girl, how the hellers be damned are you, you little minx. I say, you look absolutely ravishing young lady. Give me forty years and I would be in with a chance along with those village boys.' He swayed as he spoke the words and Rosie wondered if he was about to fall over backward.

'You be in with more chance than thems village boys Fenston you handsome devil.' She stood on the end of her toes and reached up to kiss Lord Crowthorn on the cheek. 'You be lookin in a good mood Mr. Crowthorn, I mean Lord Crowthorn. You be feeling good today or sumpin?'

'No, no, call be Fenston young lady. And yes, I am in an absolute hooting stonker of a grand mood. Spiffingly good mood, dare I say.' Rosie could sense that she had hit the jackpot today, but she did not want to rush in too quickly.

'Oh, that be right, Fenston. Well, tell me then you handsome old thing. What be giving you the good mood?' Lord Crowthorn managed to straighten up, a look of utter pride written across his face. He even looked sober and younger as he said the words.

'Rosie, my dear little lady. Today, yes today, the Christmas present I purchased for my dear wife Lady Elizabeth has arrived. It sits in the old garage shed near the outbuildings. Mr. Specto Specteraldow Roony the Speckter is keeping it safe for me. Oh, she will be so happy when she sees it.' Lord Crowthorn was now almost jumping up and down as he said the words. He could hardly contain his excitement. 'Would you like to see it, Rosie? Oh, please tell me you would like to see it.' The housemaid sighed; this was proving to be more work than she expected.

'Corse, I would like to be seeing it Fenston. Corse, I would.' She followed the excited Lord Crowthorn to the sheds at the rear of the house. He, staggering and dancing his way along while the young woman followed him.

'Well, what do you think Rosie? Is it not just the most spiffing present a man could ever give to his love? Tell me she will adore it, Rosie, tell me.' Rosie stared at the present sat in front of her. It was hard to tell whether she adored it or not as she stood in silence looking at it.

'Er, yes, corse she gonna loves it Fenston. How nice of you. I wish I had a husband what gived me such presents. No money and no presents, that's poor little Rosie Thresher, that be my lot spose.' She looked down at the floor to complete the act and then stood on her toes again to give Lord Crowthorn his customary peck on the cheek. 'Bet be goin now Fenston. Not got much to do tonight, will have to stay in.'

'Why Rosie, surely a gorgeous young lady like you will have a queue of village boys waiting to take you out?'

'Not be that Fenston. It be not having no money to get me something nice to wear. Wages in Elphinstone be only enough to give my mam. She leave me with nothin, not a bean. Wish I had a man like you to looks after me, Fenston.' It suddenly dawned on Lord Crowthorn that in his excitement over the Christmas present, he had forgotten to play the game. The same one the young woman concocted every time they met.

'Why, someone as adorable as you Rosie should always have the best.' He reached into his tweed jacket and pulled out a wad of notes.

'O thankee, thankee Fenston, you are so lovely. Why you must be the handsomest man I has ever knowd.' She gave him another peck on the cheek and headed off, the notes clutched firmly in her hand. Rosie knew that Lord Fenston was so distracted and drunk he had given her far more than he usually would. She walked away from the building making sure to wait until she was out of sight before counting it. Suddenly she heard Lord Crowthorn shout her name, *shit, he must have realised he has given me too much.* Rosie turned around in disappointment.

'Rosie, do you, do you really think that Lady Elizabeth will love her spiffing Christmas present?' Rosie laughed to herself before shouting her reply.

'She gonna wet herself with joy when she see that, Fenston.' With that final comment, Rosie turned and walked off into the chill afternoon to count her money.

With only a few weeks to go until Christmas Lady Crowthorn was feeling excited. No, not about the spiffing present from Lord Crowthorn, she knew nothing about that yet. The excitement came from having something to do other than the usual. It was the fun of putting up the tree, decorating the large house and preparing for visitors.

Her daughter Heather Bowfield Lachlan Browning would be arriving from Scotland at noon on Christmas day. The grandchildren Steven Thomas, Rempton Flavel, and Lilly Sumpton Camarg would be with her. The youngsters were not yet teenagers, but Elizabeth knew that this might be the last time all of them would come for the annual visit. She loved her daughter and the grandchildren but was not keen on him, Spencer Bowfield Lachlan Browning. Well, that is not totally true. Lady Crowthorn could have put up with her daughter's boring husband but she knew that it would only take a few hours before Lord Crowthorn became openly hostile to him. It happened every year no matter how hard he tried to not get agitated. The problem was a very difficult one, most horrendous for Fenston to deal with. Simply horrific in fact. You see Spencer Bowfield Lachlan Browning had that annoying habit of being tea total. He had never been in a pub in his life, something he was very proud of. According to Fenston, his son in law was an *Alien from hell and a frightful bore to match.*

Lady Crowthorn continued to edge around the side of the house. She was doing her weekly check on the work the gardener had done and as usual she was not happy with his efforts. For some reason, she decided to go and look for him and assumed he might be doing his usual. Hiding and having a smoke in one of the old outbuildings. Now don't ask me why, call it a woman's intuition but she started to walk towards the old garage. Lady Crowthorn was just about to pull open the rotting wooden door when she nearly did wet herself as old Brendon Speckler tapped her on the shoulder from behind. 'Be not wantin to go in thur M'lady.'

'Oh, for Christ's sake Mr. Speckler, you gave me a frightful start there. What do you mean by sneaking up on me like that?' She took a deep breath in the cold damp morning air and tried to compose herself.

'Anyway, what do you mean, I do not want to go in there? I do want to go in there and now you have told me that I do not want to go in there, then I want to go in there even more.'

'Be not wantin to go in there cos it be a secret what Lord tells me.'

'Mr. Speckler, what on earth are you talking about? Why would Fenston want to hide anything from me? What on earth is that man up to now?' The gardener was in a tricky position. He had been sworn to keep the secret until Christmas day but now he had no choice but to tell the lady of the house or at least keep her from looking inside.

'It be your Christmas present, M'lady. His Lordship tells me to keep it hid till Christmas day. Be shame if you does ruin his surprise.' Lady Crowthorn could not hide the warm feeling of joy that was sweeping over her. A big smile started to form across her face and her whole body became relaxed with contentment.

'Why Mr. Speckler, how lovely of you to try and keep this a secret. Of course, I will not look. This is positively the most wonderous thing Lord Crowthorn could have done for me.' In her unbridled excitement, she leaned forward and kissed the old gardener on the cheek before turning and strutting away, a delighted woman. Brendon Speckler stood there in shock. Well when I say in shock, I mean slightly confused. He did not do emotion, but it was unheard of for the Lady of the house to be so informal with him. The gardener shook his head before lighting another cigarette and muttered under his breath.

'Lady L'beth been married to him too long. She turnin into a fuckin nut ball as well.'

Of course, it would prove to be impossible for the Lady of the house to hide her joy from Lord Crowthorn for long. It was only a few days later that she confronted him. Fenston was just about to amble down the road, a fifteen-minute walk timed perfectly to co-inside with The Black oak opening at mid-day. 'Fenston my darling, could I just have a quick word before you meet the boys?' He turned around with a look of concern written on his face. She never held him up while he was engaged on important pub business.

'Yes, my love, my ship floating on the ocean of dreams, my flower blooming in the winter sun, my sweet potato gathered in the harvest, my...'

'Fenston, will you shut up just for a moment. My love, I know about the present you got me.' Lord Crowthorn went white with shock.

'Oh, sweet woman. Have you seen it, please tell me have not seen it yet?'

'No, no I have not seen it Fenston. Mr. Speckler stopped me just as I was about to go into the garage. He told me you want to wait until Christmas day. I just want to say, well, thank you Fenston, I really do love you.' Fenston smiled at her, just a quick smile though as he had now lost a few minutes drinking time.

'You will love it, Lizzie. Why it is positively the most spectacular present any woman could ever wish for.' Then he turned back towards the direction of the Black Oak and skipped down the road.

It was the day before Christmas eve when the miracle happened. I suppose you could call the day before Christmas eve, Christmas eve of eve or Christmas eve minus one or Christmas, oh you know what I mean. Let us just say it was two days before Christmas day that the wonderous phenomenon occurred. It would forever be known in local folklore as the Elphinstone trip. They had talked about it for a full week before but no one in the group thought of it as anything more than drunken pub chatter. Lord Crowthorn had been serious of course, very serious. The main credit for the miracle had to go to the Landlord of The Black Oak, Geoff Stannerwix. He had finally convinced the gang to go along with the visit by offering to drive them up to the large house in his van after 2 p.m. closing time. To get agreement from everyone he had promised to open the pub early on their return after the trip. The deal had been cemented when Fenston also offered a free bar for them all that evening.

Old Brendon Speckler was waiting as agreed at the top of the driveway of Elphinstone House. Lord Crowthorn stepped carefully from the passenger seat in the van. He looked furtively around as if he was a secret agent on a daring mission. There were two reasons for this odd behaviour, he was worried in case Lady Crowthorn had not gone into town as planned and the other reason? He was drunk as a Lord. I mean even more drunk than usual. Put it down to excitement because of the visit and the eight pints he had consumed in little more than two hours.

'Speck the Spectacular, you old fruit. Give me a hug old boy, has she gone as planned?' The gardener backed off before Fenston could grab him in a drunken bear hug.

'Be gone to town as be said she wuz M'lord.' Fenston clapped his hands together like an excited schoolboy.

'Topper Whizzo Mr. Spack Spock Spuckter, just absolutely top ho.'

While Lord Crowthorn was conducting his drunken recourse with the bemused gardener, Geoff Stannerwix was opening the back doors to the van. He tried not to laugh at the site of the five bodies heaped together in the back. He used the van to stock his pub, so it had no rear seats. The drunken passengers had been bouncing about as he drove them to Elphinstone House. Tony the taxi was first out. 'Could you not have driven a bit slower you fucking lunatic Stannerwix?' Next came Robbie Glander, his bald head covered in sweat.

'Forkin mad man Stannerwix, forkin madman. It be good job you openin the pub early cos otherwise I might have belted ye.' The comment from the small and slightly built Glander twin caused much laughter from the others as they scrambled out one by one. Geoff Stannerwix was a big man and he could have probably lifted Robbie Glander with one arm.

Lord Crowthorn ambled around to the back of the van to address the assembled drunken party. The gardener leaned on his rake while watching, just a hint of a smile on his lips. 'Ok boys, attention, ATTENTION'. Fenston shouted the words out as though he was a sergeant addressing his troops.

'Fucking get on with it will you Feni, it is fucking freezing out here. The quicker we get this crazy visit over with then the quicker we can get back to the pub.' The words from Tobi Clusterball Glander were met with more laughter. The party were really all enjoying this most unusual trip and of course, the icing on the cake would be the extra few hours they had earned in the pub on their return.

'Now, let us just check one last final time. Not a word, not a jolly bean from any of you. In fact, I want you all to raise your hand and swear to say nothing of Lady Elizabeth's super prezzy wezzy until she sees it on Christmas day. Repeat after me. I swear...' The assembled party ignored him and started to walk after the gardener towards the old outbuildings.

'Shut the fuck up Feni, we want to see this bloody present you have been going on about for weeks. Plus, it is fecking freezing out here, stop pissing around and let us see what it is.' Toni said the words with affection rather than any real malice. Lord Crowthorn was giggling with excitement as he followed his friends as they stumbled towards the dilapidated garage.

The van bounced around on the gravel path as it headed back to the village. Lord Crowthorn felt rather unwell. It was probably the motion of the vehicle added to the copious amount of beer he had consumed. He and the driver were separated by the steel panel so they could only vaguely hear the passengers in the back as well as not being able to see them. For once Crowthorn tried to be serious and act like the sixty-nine-year-old adult he was. Fenston looked at Geoff Stannerwix with pleading eyes, almost as though he was afraid of getting the wrong answer. 'Geoff, Geoff old boy. Be honest with me, I mean be brutal if you need to be old chap. Tell me the truth. Do you think Lady Elizabeth will like her Christmas present? Oh, please tell me she will be delighted Geoff, please tell me. But be honest, tell me the truth, oh do say she will simply adore it.' Geoff turned his eyes off the road ahead for a few moments, making the excited adult child wait a few moments before giving his answer.

'Feni old boy, she is going to be dancing in the fucking hallway when she sees that present. Trust me on that one Crowthorn, trust me.' Fenston clasped his hands together with utter glee even though he was feeling rather sickly, a small pain gathering in his chest.

'Oh, I just knew you would say that Geoff. I just knew it. Oh God, I wish it was Crimpers day today, Lizzie is going to be simply topper with glee, absolutely top ho jolly jumpers when she sees it. I just can't wait. I say, old boy, get a move on. I really could do with a pint.'

As the van lurched from side to side the five occupants in the back sat silently. They seemed to be in shock, it was Rufus O'Callaghan who spoke first. 'Do you think his old lady is going to like it then?' No one spoke for a few seconds and then Glib Paddering started laughing. Slowly the rest joined in. That kind of laugh where you cannot stop even when it becomes painful. In the front of the van, Lord Crowthorn could just make out the sound of the joyful hilarity in the back. That was all he needed to tell him that the present really was the most spiffingly wonderful gift a man could ever get for his wife.

Christmas morning had arrived, December 25th was back again and Fenston felt positively ill as he woke from his drunken sleep. This was the one day of the year that Lord Crowthorn hated with a passion. There were two reasons for this, both blindingly obvious if you have been paying attention to the story so far. The first was the visit from the Lachlan Brownings. Of course, Fenston loved seeing his daughter Heather Bowfield and he could even put up with her annoying offspring, Steven Thomas, Rempton Flavel and that other little tyke Lilly Sumpton Camarg. No, it was him, that none drinking big pain in the arse, Spencer Bowfield Lachlan Browning. Lord Crowthorn hated him even more than he disliked Christmas.

The second reason he hated this particular day of the year, the pub was closed. Holy sweet mother of all that is sacred, how on earth was Fenston expected to cope with such horror. But of course, he did cope, and do you know how? He just drank double in the Black Oak on Christmas Eve. That was why he felt worse than usual on Christmas morning.

Lord Crowthorn staggered out of his bed and started

to get dressed. It was nearly eleven a.m. and the dreaded visitors would be arriving at midday. Fenston felt odd, ok he had his usual hangover that would normally be cured with a visit to the pub. Something else was wrong, it was the pain in his chest. It had been niggling him for a week and would not go away. *Dashed strange little blighter, I wonder what it is? Maybe that sandwich I had yesterday evening, cheese a little too strong for the old tummy. I know what will sort it out.* Lord Crowthorn walked over to the bedroom table and poured himself a large whisky and lit up a king-sized cigar.

He was positively bouncing down the large staircase. The half bottle of morning whisky had done the trick and now the time had arrived. 'Elizabeth, Lizzy, where the damned are you girl. It is time to see your most wonderful present. Oh, where on earth are you woman?' Fenston went running out to the front of the large mansion expecting to find his missing wife but the only person he could see was the old gardener leaning on his rake as usual.

'My dear Spic the Spookter, have you seen the lady of the house, oh pray you will say yes. Come on old Spakaroono the specky head, where are you hiding her?'

'Be not hidin hur any wurs Lord Crowthorn. Be her waitin at the outbuildings, be thinkin she wants to see hur present, but I tell hur to be waitin for you.'

'Oh Mr. Spunkster, you are an absolute love. Wait here for me while I run around to the old garage. What a top lad you really are old Spacker Spocker Spunkface.' Fenston grabbed the old gardener before he could back off and gave him a big slobbering kiss on the forehead. He then jogged off in his usual drunken zig-zag fashion to find his wife. Brendon shook his head and laughed before turning to lean on his garden rake again. Just before Lord Crowthorn disappeared around the side of the house he heard the shouted words,

'Oh, and a very merry Christmas to you Mr. Spocko Spack Spudster.'

'Same bein to you, you fucking lunatic.' But of course, Brendon said his reply softly to make sure his master could not hear him.

'Lizzy, oh Lizzy, thank sweet Jesus you waited for me. Are you excited, oh tell me you are excited, dear girl?' Lady Crowthorn laughed, she knew he was drunk again but did not care. Elizabeth was even preparing to forgive him for the fall out he would no doubt have later on that day with their son in law. No, today she was a happy woman. It did not even matter that much to her what the present was. What mattered was, he, yes him, Fenston had at long last thought of someone else other than himself. Maybe this was the first sign of him growing up. He was still acting like a child but at least he was excited about giving her something. She wondered if it was a new car, it had to be big if it was stored in the old garage.

'Of course, I am excited you, silly man. It has been driving me positively crackers trying to keep from sneaking a look. Come on Fenston, can I see it now?' Lord Crowthorn hopped up and down with joy before pulling his scarf from around his neck.

'No, no, not so quick. This deserves to wait, my dear. You will positively love it. Oh, I just know you will. You need to put my scarf around your eyes so that you get to see your present when I switch on the light, my love.' Lady Crowthorn shook her head with impatience but she was enjoying the playful excitement to the build-up for what she was now certain must be a new car.

'Hurry up then Fenston, your daughter and her family will be here any moment.'

'Oh God my sweetest, don't remind me.' Lord Crowthorn said the words without even a hint of malice. He was so happy about the upcoming surprise.

The blindfold was now on and Lady Crowthorn could feel Fenston's hands on her shoulders as he guided her towards the garage. They walked like one of those pantomime horses, he pissed as a newt and her unable to see a thing.

'Just a few more steps Lizzy, just a few....aaaargh.' She could no longer feel him holding her although she had heard a bang and assumed, he was opening the garage door.

'Fenston, what are you doing? Fenston, Fenston?' Elizabeth took a few more steps forward and then crashed straight into the still-closed doors. Her head bounced off the rotting wood before she stumbled backward and fell onto the gravel path. Even though she was dazed and still on the ground Lady Crowthorn managed to pull off the blindfold.

'Fenston, Fenston, what is going on?'

'Be nuthin going on M'Lady. Be no heart doin no nuthin. Think ee be dead M'Lady.' Brendon was standing over the body of Lord Crowthorn who lay spread-eagled on the ground, his face white and lifeless.

'I watched him M'Lady, I think he tooks a heart attack. I should get a doctur, but I thinkin the Lord be passed any docturin. He be deader than my old mam and she be gone twenty-year past.'

Lady Crowthorn staggered to her feet and was staring at the prostrate body of her late husband with a mixture of shock and confusion. To make matters worse she could hear the car wheels of the Lachlan Browning's crunching on the gravel road. Now I know you are going to think of her as being rather callous but amid all this chaos she could only think of one thing. It was not giving her husband the kiss of life; he was beyond that now anyway. No, it was the present, she wanted to see what the surprise was.

Elizabeth turned around and stumbled towards the still-closed garage door. She did not even make any attempt to wipe the mud and grass stains from her best Christmas frock. If you had been watching her you might have thought, she was a zombie. The lady of the house pulled open the stiff old wooden doors and fumbled for the light. Just before the electricity came racing down the cables and into the bulb, she could just make out the large dark shape that stood in front of her. And then the light-flooded into her eyes, blinding the old lady who stood there, staring at it like a stone-cold statue. She did not move for a least a few minutes until finally, she came to her senses. Lady Crowthorn walked around to the side of the large wooden object to see what the gold engraved sign that was attached to it said.

To My Dearest wife Elizabeth. The day you told me that I have never given you a present broke my heart. If you should go first, then it shall be yours my darling. And if I should expire before you, why then you don't even need to go and buy one.

Lady Crowthorn smiled and then started laughing. It could have been mirth or hysteria, to be honest, I was not sure. All I remember is watching this old lady standing beside a large wooden coffin that was mounted on two metal stands while outside the gardener Brendon Speckler shook his head in resignation.

HARMONICA SEEKS PARTNER

<u>Five days until Christmas</u>

Old Roddy Mackintosh turned the key slowly before taking the utmost care to ease his way down each of the three steps. Age not only makes you slower, but it also forces you to go slower in case you have that dreaded fall. Anything other than considered deliberation for every single move could lead to disaster. That was how his friend Tommy had gone, a simple fall. He had been helped up, dusted down and off he trundled. Two days later? Dead, dead as a discarded old cigarette end dropped in the gutter. *Was that not how Madge, his Madge had gone as well?* A trip, a bang. All it had been was a broken arm, but she never recovered. Of course, it did not help that she was in her eighties, but it was the fall that took her, yes, the fall. Maybe she was glad to be gone, threw herself at the pavement rather than listen to Roddy moaning anymore. *No, it was not that, it had to be the fall, yes, the fall did it.*

The rain, the incessant wet miserable drizzle was coming down again. Roddy truly believed that the rain gods waited for him to go for his daily walk to the shops. *There he goes, that miserable old bastard Mackintosh. Switch the taps on Archangel Raphael, let's get a laugh watching him moan about the weather.* But the truth was Roddy felt more at home in the deluge. Bright warm sunshine made him stand out, made him look odd. Men would be flexing their tanned muscles in t-shirts while the women strode past with their long legs exposed to the rays. He would still have his big coat buttoned up to cover his vest, shirt, and two jumpers. *Anyway, it is harder to be negative when the sun comes out, no give me the rain any day.*

This was his daily routine, a walk to the shops, on his own, always on his own. A tin of beans each day and a bag of potatoes every three days. A loaf every two days and occasionally, very occasionally a tub of margarine. It was the cost you see; everything was far too expensive. *I remember when you could get the same shopping for two and six. Decimalisation, that's what screwed it all up. Eight pounds forty, eight bloody pound forty for a few messages. Bloody rip-*

off, it is these bloody foreigners, conning us real Scots, taking us true Brits for everything we worked for. I mean who won the bloody war? I tell you it was not the Germans and yet they live in the lap of bloody luxury.

He was turning onto the main road now, lost in his thoughts. The little shops spread out in a thin line along the busy thoroughfare. Charity stores, coffee houses, and the small supermarket. The last one was Roddy's destination. He had never been in a coffee franchise and would die before he went into a charity shop. *The money just goes into the pocket of the rich, it is all a con.* Oh, I forgot to mention, the bank. There was still one last bank where once there had been four. Old Mackintosh had no idea what he would do if it closed. He did not own a bank card and online banking, are you being serious? Once a week he would call in to pay any bills and draw out £60. That would last him the whole seven days. It used to be £50 but inflation had forced the increase. *Robbing bastards keep putting the prices up. That will be the bloody European parliament, sending the profits to be wasted on allowing lazy immigrants to have it easy in our country. We need to take Britain back, give it back to the true British, who won the bloody war anyway?*

She had seen him now, she always looked up and stared

when he was around 100 yards away. Why did she only ever lift her head when Roddy appeared? Not an exaggerated lift, just a slight incline up from the permanently bowed position she held each day. The patterned scarf would be tied tightly around her greasy white curls while the dirty black shawl would cover everything except her hands. She would sit on old newspapers with the paper cup held between her gnarled fingers. It would only be Roddy who would get a slight glimpse of the cracked face, a few broken black teeth hanging in the cavern of her mouth.

Old Mackintosh was level with her now, just before walking through the glass doors of the little supermarket. He eyed her up while she returned the glare before muttering the same old words.

'Spare pound for an old lady, spare pound kind Sir.'

Dirty scrounging beggars, go and get a job and work like the rest of us had to do. I did not fight in the war to let our country become overrun by Eastern Europeans who never worked a day in their lives.

Her eyes glared with hate as if she was reading his thoughts. The old lady would occasionally get a few coppers from the affluent locals but of course nothing from Roddy. He spent so little that both his state pension and work pension had continued to build up. Without Madge to hide the occasional luxury she had bought; the money had grown and would pass away when he died. No children and little family left, but he would never spend. No, money was to be kept not frittered away. Roddy picked up his tin of beans and headed towards the potatoes. A three-pound bag of course, never a five.

Four Days until Christmas

The first flecks of snow had begun to fall. They quickly melted into the wet ground but as the flurry continued a thin white carpet started to appear. Roddy turned slowly out of his driveway and onto the little suburban side street. 92 Frederick Avenue had been his home since he and Madge had moved there in the early nineteen-fifties. A young couple still in their mid-twenties arriving into middle-class suburbia. Had that been the start of his decline? What happened to the carefree young man who seemed to enjoy life? It was as if each day that passed allowed another tiny piece of his soul to be chipped away as he accelerated towards mortality. Now all that was left was spite and hatred but worse of all came the creeping loneliness. His friends and family had passed on or disappeared and then Madge. She was the last one, all he had left. And now all that remained was the snow and the daily trip to the little supermarket.

It took him a few minutes to walk the two hundred yards down to the junction with the main road. It was a further ten minutes from there to the shops. The snow was still light, but the cold made each of the white specks sting when they landed on bare skin. Not that the cold bothered Roddy, he just added another old jumper to the endless layers he already wore. Anyway, the snow was good, it meant she would be uncomfortable and wet, that scrounging old peasant. The thought of her suffering even more than usual pleased the old man.

You could never describe Roddy as being in a good mood. His scale only went from an awful mood to a bad mood at best. Let us just say he was at the more positive end of his own bleak measurement system this morning. Of course, it was nothing to do with it being four days until Christmas, are you being serious? No, the real reason was that this was just a beans day. Try to keep up. Remember I told you that old Mackintosh only bought a loaf every second day and potatoes every third day? Well, this was one of those rare daily shopping trips that coincided with no requirement for bread or potatoes. He would only have to part with the price of a tin of beans. Now the thing is, I don't do the shopping in my house. I have no idea how much a single tin of beans costs, but I could tell by Roddy's face that he was contemplating spending less than a pound.

But something was wrong. He had completed this trip every day without fail for the last five years. Ever since Madge had given up the ghost and moved on. Very little changed each morning as he shuffled down to the supermarket. Okay, maybe another charity shop replaced the butchers, or a bank closed and became a coffee shop. The people, they all kept to the same routine.

She had moved, maybe just slightly but that was all she needed to do to upset Roddy's structured world. The old woman had repositioned herself no more than a foot away from her usual place at the supermarket door. Now that may not have meant much to me or you but to Roddy, it was just another insult. *How dare she. The thieving lazy old witch has moved a foot closer to my house. Why did she not go to the other side of the door and then I would not have to walk past her to enter the shop? She can go where the hell she wants; it makes no difference to me. We did not win the war to end up paying the rest of Europe to send us their beggars.* But of course, it did make a difference to Roddy. The move had been executed by the old hag just to annoy him, why else would she do it?

As he edged past the old lady she looked up. He could have sworn she had a glint in her eyes as though she was laughing at him.

'Spare pound for an old lady, spare pound kind sir.'

She held up her cup as he ignored her and stumbled on. Did she seriously think old Roddy would give her a pound? That was all he had brought with him today. It would pay for the beans and he would also get some change. That could be added back into tomorrow's expenses as a triple whammy was coming up. Bread, potatoes and beans day.

The cashier took the tin from Roddy. 'Would you like a bag, Mr. Mackintosh?'

'No, no. Not since you started charging for them. I fought in the bloody war for this country and now we must pay for the shopping and the bag. It is a bloody scandal.'

Jenny the till operator tried to hide her weary smile. She knew damn well old Roddy would not buy a bag, but the shop staff all enjoyed listening to his daily moans. To them, he was a bit of free amusement. *I dare you to try and get him to mention the war three times while he pays for his tin of beans.* But today he took her by surprise by introducing a completely new subject. This was unheard of. He always said the same thing or at least meant the same thing.

'Why has that beggar woman moved from outside?' Jenny turned to look out of the large glass window.

'Has she? I did not notice. Oh, she looks to be in the same place to me. She always sits at that spot.' Jenny returned her gaze to old Roddy.

'No, no, she has changed places from her usual position. The old ba…I mean woman usually sits right beside the door. Now she is a foot further over, can't you see, look, look.' Roddy's thinly disguised irritation failed miserably as he almost spat the words out.'

'That will be 87 pence please, Mister Mackintosh.' Jenny had quickly tired of talking to old Roddy. It was fun when he moaned but his obsession with the old beggar woman and her supposed move seemed weird to her. She could feel his bigotry and hatred seeping out and was afraid he would go too far.

'Well, maybe she has just moved a little bit to give people more room as they come through the door.' Jenny looked up at Roddy and smiled before continuing.

'We sometimes take her a coffee or a cake out, she is

a poor old soul. Have a lovely Christmas, Mr. Mackintosh.'

But Roddy was already shuffling out of the shop. *The old hag is a freeloader. Probably came over as an illegal immigrant and now these idiots are giving her free stuff from the shops. No wonder prices are so bloody expensive. I fought in the war for these people and I still have to pay my way. That is all the gratitude I get for serving my country.'*

<u>Three days until Christmas</u>

The snow was now a few inches thick and continued to fall. Even the suburban houses of Frederick Avenue had taken on a Christmas card look as the white powder lay its blanket over the earth.

Old Roddy searched through the drawer in the damp bedroom for another jumper to add to the two he wore every day. She had kept things organised, folded his clothes neatly away, matched his socks, cleaned and polished the house. Now the layer of dust inside the building was almost as thick as the snow outside. He tried not to think about Madge, it brought on the slightest feeling of guilt. He knew he should have appreciated her more. At one time he had, so many years ago but age, time and familiarity breed contempt. In her last years, they hardly spoke. Almost as if time and routine meant words no longer mattered. They each understood their position and accepted their lot while waiting for Father Time to pay his last visit.

This was one of those days when his mood really did match the biting cold outside. It was bad enough having to turn the gas fire on. God forbid, it was also that point when the moon and the sun aligned to black out the earth. Yes, it was beans, potatoes and loaf day. And to make matters even worse, the supermarket would close on Christmas day. That meant that either today or tomorrow he would need to buy double groceries. Roddy felt like weeping as he contemplated having to spend so much. *I fought in the bloody war and they set up free food banks for these scrounging foreigners.* Roddy could have gone to a food bank himself I suppose but pride would never allow him to do that. Oh, and the eighty thousand pounds he had in the bank that would remain untouched until he left this earth.

Roddy stared with disbelief at the shape sitting with the black shawl draped over its shoulders. The flecks of snow had started to settle on the old woman as she sat on the freezing pavement. She was facing out onto the main road as it made its junction with Frederick Avenue. He wanted to stop and scream at her, aim a kick, push her out into the morning traffic as it crawled through the slush. He held his gaze as straight as possible as he turned the corner to pass her.

'Spare pound for an old lady, spare pound kind sir.'

He did not look but he knew she was laughing at him. The few feet she had moved yesterday had just been a precursor to her setting up at the end of his street. *Damn you, you old witch. Well, you can move closer to my house all you want. I don't care; I hope you freeze to death you old bag.*

But no matter how much he tried to convince himself to the contrary, it was no good. She had upset the equilibrium, ruined his routine. As he walked through the doors of the supermarket, he could feel her absence. Even worse, he would have to pass her again on the way home. Roddy shook the snow from his old raincoat and reluctantly lifted a shopping basket. A sure sign that he was going to have to buy more than a tin of beans today.

'That will be £11.45 please Mr. Mackintosh.' Jenny had geared herself up for the usual rant about the price of things from the old man. In fact, she expected a heavy tirade as this was more than he had ever spent in the past. She tried to make a joke of things but instantly regretted the words.

'You have a lot of shopping today, Mr. Mackintosh, are you expecting visitors?'

'What, what do you mean? No, no visitors. No one ever visits, ever, not ever.' She sensed that the old man was not really listening to her. He seemed to be looking back at the entrance to the little supermarket.

'She has moved, moved to the end of my road. The old woman, why?' Jenny stared in surprise.

'Oh, has she. I wondered why she was not here today; I was worried about her. She must have been late coming out as well. I walked down passed Frederick Avenue only half an hour ago and she was not there. This is my late start day; I must look after my little boy until my husband gets back from his shift. Do you need a bag, Mr. Mackintosh?'

'Yes, yes, I will take a bag as well.' Jenny looked at him with shock written across her face.

Roddy slowly shuffled up the main road as the snow continued to fall. The new shopping bag held firmly in his hand with his recently acquired groceries. The old woman was watching him in the distance as he crunched through the white powder. The world was changing, his world was changing. First, the old hag had moved her begging position and now he had purchased a plastic bag. His body felt clammy and sweaty inside the layers of clothing despite the intense cold. She was unnerving the old man, winning the battle but not the war. *I fought for the freedom of this country from the likes of you. We won the war and we will win again to take our country back for the true British people.*

Two days until Christmas

He stood transfixed at the window. The curtains just slightly pulled apart in case she turned around and saw where he lived. But no matter how many times he closed them and then peered out again, she was still there. Sitting with her back to him on the pavement. The black shawl covering her back, the thin white strands of her dirty hair flowing out from the patterned headscarf. He contemplated calling the police but wondered if they charged you for the call? Anyway, what was he going to say? *Hello, can you get me the police?*

What is the problem, Sir?

The beggar woman, she moved to the end of my street and now she has moved again.

Oh dear, ok Sir, can you tell me exactly where she has moved to?

Yes, I bloody well can. She has moved to right outside my house. She is sitting on the pavement with her paper cup beside her. Begging and freeloading as usual. It is a bloody disgrace, I fought in the war for...

Oh, dear Sir, that is awful. Stay exactly where you are, and we will send an armed response unit round immediately.

Even old Roddy knew he would be laughed at. No, the only thing to do was to just act normal and go about his daily routine. He had used his new bag yesterday to get double groceries. *Maybe today he would just buy one last tin of beans just to give him an excuse to go to the shops.* Something was wrong though, no not just the old hag outside. It was something else. He did not feel that slight hint of satisfaction he usually got when it was a single tin day. He should have felt pleased that the day of spending less than a pound had come around but somehow it did not seem to matter anymore.

He opened the money tin and counted out the coins. And then he tipped them all into his pocket. Roddy locked the front door and trundled past the old hag while trying his best to ignore the words that would inevitably come.

'Spare pound for an old lady, spare pound kind Sir.'

But he was unnerved even though he did not want to

admit it. *A beggar outside his house, what on earth was the world coming to. This was the fault of the government; I mean who won the bloody war anyway?* But he cheered up when the snow started to fall even harder, and the biting wind cut in. He had four jumpers on under his coat now. He hoped the old lady would suffer even more in the cold. That would serve her right for begging not only in his street but right outside his home. *The bloody cheek.*

And yet, the odd thing was, even though Roddy was saying those words in his head, he did not really feel them. He did not understand why the old beggar was playing games with him but somehow it did not matter anymore. He had nothing, nothing but snow and emptiness and loneliness. The hag was trying to get to him but at least it was him. Roddy shuffled on down the road and even contemplated buying something other than beans, bread, and potatoes for a change. *Madge used to buy biscuits. Maybe I shall buy a packet of digestive biscuits, just a small packet.* The world was changing, getting smaller. The snow continued to fall until a white silence encircled those who still lived and breathed.

<u>Christmas Eve</u>

Old Roddy turned over in his bed. The daylight was penetrating through the dark curtains and he knew the alarm would be going off shortly. After 87 years force of habit meant that he woke at roughly the same time each day. He set the alarm for 7:30 am but rarely would he need it to go off. Maybe it was a good thing? At his age, the clanging of the ancient old alarm clock might give him a heart attack.

Now I bet some of you are clicking away on your calculator trying to catch me out. Let's say this story was written in 2018 and the writer says Mr. Mackintosh is 87. So, 2018 minus 87 means he was born in 1931. The war started in 1939 so you are telling me he was conscripted into the army at the age of 8! Call yourself an author. You really need to work out your plotlines Mr. Pearson. If you want to be taken seriously as a writer, then get your sums right. I bet Ernest Hemingway never fucked up the continuity in his stories the way you do.

But you have jumped the gun dear reader. I never said that old Mackintosh fought in the war. It was he who went on about it. The fact was he had never seen any real action. Roddy did his national service after the war ended but most of it was spent in the army band. He had once been a mean harmonica player. Oh yes, at one time Mr. Mackintosh had enjoyed life but slowly he retreated into his own bleak world until his sole joy became a beans only day.

He dressed slowly, trousers, socks, a second pair of socks, a vest, four jumpers and finally the coat. If it had been possible, he would have put on jumper number five. He did try, but it would not fit over the others. He peered out of his bedroom window at the thick driving snow and smiled. *Surely even she has moved back to a more sheltered spot than outside my front door.*

As always, old Roddy was right. She had indeed moved to a more sheltered spot as the old lady was now sitting in the middle of his living room. Even though she was inside she still sat on the carefully placed newspapers with her black shawl covering her thin body. She looked up and gave the slightest of smiles as she exposed the last few black teeth she had left.

'Spare pound for an old lady, spare pound kind Sir.'

The old man simply ignored her and went into the kitchen to get the money. The packet of biscuits stood like a statue on the small table with the new plastic bag folded neatly beside them. Outside the snow continued to fall and was starting to drift up against the side of the house. Roddy felt strange, he felt different, something new had happened. It was the biscuits, they made him feel good. Not because he had tasted them, the packet was unopened. No, it was because they were there, in his house. Something to distract him from the incessant loneliness. The biscuits, the plastic bag, new friends to join the beans, the bread, the potatoes, and the snow. Ok, the old beggar had taken over his living room but to hell with her. Roddy was not going to give her what she wanted, she could sit there forever if she felt like it. *She was getting fuck all from him.*

He turned the key in the back door and headed with caution out into the snow. He was sure that she would be gone when he came back. One day when the health visitor came, he had to wait until after 2 pm to go to the shops and the old hag was not there. Roddy assumed that she went home in the afternoons, a part-time scrounger. *She must beg on the early shift. I fought in the bloody war and she only works for half of the day. These immigrants, don't know how lucky they are.*

Jenny looked up and smiled at Roddy as she handed him the tin of beans. 'That will be 69 pence, Mr. Mackintosh.'

'69 pence, it was 87 pence a tin yesterday. Did you overcharge me?'

'No Mr. Mackintosh, they are on a special offer today. We are clearing stock out before we close for Christmas.' Jenny handed the old man his 31 pence change and then she looked on in stunned amazement. Roddy took the change and without saying a word he slowly placed the coins into the charity box that stood on the counter beside the till operator. She watched him in silence as his stooped frame walked back through the automatic doors and disappeared into the swirling white mass outside.

Christmas Day

Roddy was still in that half-sleep state just before you open your eyes and wake up. His brain had kicked into gear to think about getting up and the day ahead, but he was still not quite aware of his surroundings. *Bloody Christmas day. The shops will be shut, what will I do all day?*

But even though his eyes remained closed he was aware that something was not right. The bed felt different; the covers did not enclose his body the way they usually did. It was as if something was making them feel loose. And then he heard it, breathing, a croaking hoarse intake of air as though each gasp was a battle. Old Mackintosh opened his eyes and turned in horror to stare at the face lying next to him in the bed. She looked into his eyes, her mouth open to show the black teeth, her foul breath sweeping over him. Every inch of her face was covered in cracks and lines, the thin wisps of white hair falling from beneath the patterned headscarf.

'Spare pound for an old lady, spare pound kind sir.'

Roddy sighed with resignation and climbed out of the bed. He put on his old dressing gown and walked into the kitchen before taking down the money tin. His bony fingers picked up the pound coin, the motion taking far more effort than it should have. He shuffled back into the bedroom and handed the old lady the coin. She smiled at him, her face becoming younger in her moment of triumph. The beggar woman climbed out of the bed and reached inside her shawl. Her frail hand re-appeared holding the Christmas cake Jenny had given her yesterday. He looked at the woman for the first time as a human being rather than a scrounger. But kindness had not been in his soul for so long that he did not know where to go next. So, he said the only words his brain could come up with in that awkward moment of respect.

'Do you know that I used to play the harmonica?'

Jenny continued transferring napkins, plates, cutlery, everything onto the dining table. Her husband Andrew swung the toddler up and down by the arms. The child giggling and screaming with excitement at every rise and fall.

'Did I tell you that the old beggar woman disappeared two days before I finished for Christmas?'

'Oh, that old lady, the one who sits on the newspapers outside the store? Oh, I liked her, what happened to her, Jen?'

'I heard a rumour she passed away that day. They found the body in the hall of the place she lived in. It seemed she stayed on her own down in one of the flats at Waverley Gardens.' Jenny folded the paper napkins over at each table setting before continuing.

'The staff will miss her. We used to take her coffee and cakes out at lunchtime. She was a right old chatterbox. I don't know if it was all true, but she used to tell us she was a Polish resistance fighter during the second world war. Supposedly she was given UK citizenship after she helped British soldiers escape from the Nazis. Of course, we took it all with a pinch of salt but at least she was a cheery old soul. That old guy, Mr. Macintosh hated her. I could tell by the way he looked at her.' Andrew laughed at hearing the name.

He was used to Jenny talking about how miserable the old man was.

'Does he still come in each day and buy one tin of beans?'

'No, I told you. Sometimes he buys bread and potatoes as well. The odd thing was, yesterday he put his change into the charity box. He took me by surprise, it was so unlike him. God, I dread getting old if that is what we have to look forward to.'

Andrew lifted the toddler into the air one more time as all three laughed and looked forward to the day ahead.

Outside the snow was drifting against the houses. Frozen spikes of ice hung from the roofs as the sun hid behind the thick grey sky. The world was changing, and everyone was growing older.

<u>Boxing Day</u>

92 Frederick Avenue was the only house with no light shining from it. A blanket of snow covered every inch of the path up to the front step. No attempt had been made to fight against the white army. No steam rose from the roof to show that the heating had joined the battle. The glass of the

windows was frosted with deadly ice.

Old Roddy and the beggar woman lay wrapped in each other's arms in the large bed. Their cold dead bodies entombed together in the damp frozen house. Directly above them in the attic was a crumbling cardboard box surrounded by the clutter of discarded life. Inside the box was an old harmonica with the words, Roddy you are my soul mate. Love, Madge 1958.

AUTUMN
(FADE OUT)

Without stating the obvious there are two parts to the season of Autumn, early and late. The contrast between the two could not be more startling. It starts with the browning of the leaves and slow wilting of the plants, a flash of vibrant golden colour so beautiful it is breath-taking. We are still basking in the glow of the fading summer, embracing nature, in love. Autumn ends with bare trees, dead plants mixed in with the dirty wet brown earth. Winter is knocking at our door and nature is no longer a lover.

I was lucky enough to be able to retire from what I call my proper job when I was still relatively young at 54. To be honest, after 30 years of stress my initial plan was to take six months out and then go and find another company that could utilise my skills. I had my fun and then the time came to go back to work. A previous colleague of mine organised an interview for me with a major company and to be honest, I was pretty much assured that I would get the job. I hope that does not sound arrogant; it is simply a statement of fact. I was no superstar but after 30 years I suppose I had the experience to do the role they offered me, in my sleep. And that leads me nicely on to what happened next.

The night before the interview I lay in my bed worrying, unable to sleep. My concern was not the interview, I was a master at them. I knew I would walk it. But that was the problem. I did not want to go back to the stress of having hundreds of people blaming me for the companies failings. And then I had one of those life-changing light bulb moments. It sounds like a cliché, but I promise you, it was real. I called my colleague and cancelled the interview. He was not happy, and we have not spoken since. I then called my wife and told her I was selling my car and buying a van and some equipment. ' What the fuck are you talking about Richard, you are supposed to be at a job interview.'

'I have changed my mind. I am going to start up my own business.' There was a confused silence at the other end of the phone before my long-suffering partner spoke again.

'Doing what?'

'I am going to become a gardener.'

'A What!!'

'I am going to dig gardens, cut grass and enjoy my own company.'

So, what has all this to do with autumn, I hear you ask? Well stick with me and I will get to the point. It was during my three years of shovelling dirt and picking up weeds that I got to meet the Autumn people. To be more precise, they were the late Autumn people. Very late in fact.

My patch covered the affluent Southern borders of Glasgow. Large old houses with big well-kept gardens. Double garages, sometimes treble and expensive cars sitting doing nothing. I remember well the nerves I had when I went to give my first quote. Years of dealing with company clients and yet I was terrified at the thought of telling someone how much it would cost to visit their garden every two weeks. I rang the bell to the large house while surveying the still lovely but slightly overgrown hedges and bushes. The door edged open and there stood Mr. James Kasela, a neat medium-sized man probably in his early eighties. The first of many late Autumn customers held out his hand in welcome. His eyes shone brightly through his worn lined face. He seemed overjoyed to see me, far happier than I expected from someone simply wanting their garden looked after.

Over those first few months of gathering customers, a pattern developed. They all had similar stories to tell. Either it was the man who answered the door and told me he was a carer for his wife who had dementia, or the woman would open the door and tell me her husband had passed away. Every one of them felt trapped in their house. Too frail to do the garden or no time as they looked after their elderly spouse. None of them cared about how much it would cost, the only question they had was, 'Will you look after my garden son, I just can't do it anymore?'

Many of the Autumn people became my friends. They would wait for me to turn up on the appointed day each fortnight, desperate for conversation. A break from the isolation of caring or being alone. My job became a mix of gardening and social care. It was both invigorating and heart-breaking. Their large houses and silent cars sat like a blanket covering them. Waiting for the moment each would finally pass away and new life would take over.

You are probably thinking, well at least these people had money, so many don't. the Autumn people had long passed the point of being envied. They would tell me they had nothing left to spend their money on. *Richard, I rarely* get out of this house, I have little I need to buy other than groceries. And yet, I am sure if you rewound 20, 30 or even 40 years ago, everyone one of them worked and saved and worried about having enough money in their old age.

We will all become Autumn people one day, I am probably closer to it than you. And then all the worries we had through life about having money, houses, cars, the latest phone, the best-kept garden, none of it will matter. We will sit alone, surrounded by our possessions, trapped. Waiting for the moment we can escape while the trinkets of life go to auction or our family. The Autumn people had reached the age were they understood this and now they only had regrets and memories of what they might have done instead. Their sad pleading eyes staring out at me from their prison. *Will you look after my garden son, I just can't do it anymore?*

Even though I no longer do gardening, I still go to visit Mr. James Kasela. He seems happier now that his wife has passed on. Of course, he misses her but at the end of her days, she became more difficult because of her dementia. He goes to the shops each day and then visits her grave. I call around to see him once a month. He enjoys seeing me but after half an hour we have nothing left to talk about and I quietly slip away. I am the only visitor he ever gets. I know that is hard to believe but it is true. Mr. James Kasela is a lovely old man. I hope that when I finally become one of the Autumn people, I will be like him. Waiting for the end with both acceptance and dignity.

BLACKBARRON

(Day 1)

The mood in the camp is good, the men are in high spirits. It is that feeling of a new beginning. Behind us is fear and oppression, ahead will be danger and possible death. The human soul was born to be free. We could have stayed, kept our heads down for a few more years and possibly survived. That is not living, surely it is better to run towards your demise than sit waiting for it?

We left Andergarth as the night moved towards dawn. Only seven of our twenty strong party are true Iceblood. The rest are Seablood and only come with us as mercenaries. I have little doubt that we could have departed the walled city during the day, but I did as she asked. I left like a scared rat, running from him, the King of The Seablood, Lord Rowallan. Thirty years as his servant, the last five as Lord Lieutenant of the City Guard. The post no doubt given to keep me and the rest of the downtrodden Iceblood in our places. Subservient to him and his people. I know she will denounce me and the rest of her kin once they realise, I have left for good. That was always my sister's plan, but how can I blame her? The marriage had at first been one of convenience. Forced on him by his father, the previous Lord Rowallan. I refuse to give them their official number after their title, it only solidifies how many thousands of years they have ruled. She took his hand to bring the two races together and yet they eventually did fall in love. Kar will always be my sister but we both knew I had to be the sacrifice. No doubt in another few years I would have been jailed or even murdered. The last Iceblood leader, the final threat to total Seablood dominance.

I drove the men on for more than twelve hours after we left. Keeping to the green fields and away from the farms and villages. We have been seen many times, but I still believe that if we are as discrete as possible then word will not get back to the walled city. The smaller the footprint we leave behind then the less chance that Rowallan will be forced to send the guard to track us down. If that happens, he will have no choice but to target me as the enemy and death will surely follow. We have 40 days to find Blackbarron as we head ever North into the Frost. I know we have to arrive well before then as we will need supplies. Food and wood to burn. Enough fire for the fifty days of black or the Ice Ghosts will take our souls. I pray that Blackbarron still stands, I pray that it even exists. It is more than 200 years since anyone has set eyes on our ancient ancestral home. If the Castle proves to be an empty rumour kept alive by Iceblood folklore, then we will die. We will be too far into the Northern Frost and the Ice Ghosts will be upon us.

(Day 2)

I would trust Serel with my life. My Captain will follow me, the heir to Blackbarron to his grave. His five Iceblood men will do the same as they too cannot return. The Seablood mercenaries are not to be trusted. They will depart our group once we reach the wildlands that edge onto The Northern Frost. From that point on there will be no return.

Even after just two days of walking the two groups split into separate camps at night. Serel has already shown open hostility to Devagan the appointed leader of the mercenaries. What choice do I have? We need them to help get us to the edge of Andergarth controlled land. The risk is that they will attack when we sleep rather than wait until I pay them. And yet both sides have everything to lose. If Devagan betrays his promise before we reach the 40th day then it will be thirteen versus seven and life will be lost on both sides.

We are less than thirty miles from the city of Andergarth and already I have relaxed. Today we started to follow the roads although as a precaution we skirted around any villages and settlements. Once we are assured of not being followed, we will need to expose our party to the locals. We will need to buy food and supplies, maybe we can even seek help from the isolated Iceblood dwellings. They will be wary of upsetting their neighbours, I understand that, but I can hope.

(Day 4)

Disaster has struck already, and I know Serel blames me for not acting. Yesterday we camped outside a small village known as Treehame. A ramshackle smattering of peasant Seablood hovels with the obligatory Inn. Devagan asked if he could take his mercenaries for wine once we had bartered for supplies. Like a fool, I agreed on the promise they would return to camp after a few hours. Maybe I already knew that they would not follow my orders, but I took the easy option to keep them on my side. Serel warned me, 'If you are giving them leeway after just three days, My Lord. What will happen in twenty or thirty days? The mercenaries are slaves to money, this will come back to haunt us.' Why am I such a fool? The Heir to Blackbarron and the Iceblood race and yet the man talking to me, Serel, is more of a King than I could ever be.

It was the shouting and running that woke me. The night was black and damp, the embers of our fire petering out. Devagan was drunk, his words incomprehensible. The men who straggled in behind him were even worse. That there had been trouble there was no doubt. We got the mercenaries into camp and let them sleep the drink off. I ordered both parties to be ready to leave as dawn broke. The Seabloods complained and when Serel attempted to kick one of them awake another fight nearly broke out. It took until after seven before we were all moving. It was only then that it became clear that they had wrecked the Inn and an unknown number of villagers had been murdered. Devagan claimed his men had been attacked by jealous locals but for once even he was quiet. Was it guilt or just a hangover?

The game was up now. I doubted that the villagers of Treehame would be able to gather enough men to take revenge, but the word would soon get back to Andergarth. Lord Rowallan would finally have his reason to send troops to finish us off once and for all. Today we have all trudged with our heads bowed. Eating up as many miles as possible between us and the fight. The two groups keeping apart, not yet open hostility but it is there, waiting to explode.

Tonight, we camped at the edge of a small forest. Superstition forcing both groups to light two fires each. Even though we are only 60 miles towards the distant Seablood border with the Northern Frost, the temperature has already fallen. A chill floats through the trees and settles into our bones. The men talk in hushed tones about the Ice Ghosts. Few have ever seen any this far South, but our fires burn anyway, just in case.

(Day 5)

I cannot believe that only five days into our journey I am making plans to break up the group and flee. We managed 20 miles today, the tired and hungover mercenaries are already asleep. We will wait until midnight and the seven true Iceblood will then break camp and run. We now have no choice after another incident on the road today.

We met a young family headed South in the hope of finding work in Andergarth. The couple had a child with them, he sat on an old donkey that was even thinner than they were. Without asking I could tell they were Iceblood peasants running from the desolate border with the Northern Frost. I wanted to tell them that they would not be welcomed the further South they travelled. Suddenly Devagan and his men surrounded the couple, they wanted the woman. Serel and his men drew their swords. It was another stand-off but once again Devagan backed down. He smiled, the smirk of a man who was biding his time before he administered death to us all. 'Calm down Serel. So quick to aid your Iceblood brethren. Put away your swords before we teach you all a lesson.' He laughed and you could feel Serel's hatred rising to a fever.

'If you touch these poor people then be prepared to die along with me, Devagan.' At this point, I jumped in between the two groups and ordered the peasants to leave. It was only then that I knew we would have to make our break with the mercenaries.

The plan had always been to part company with

Devagan once we reached the Seablood border with the Northern Frost. We hoped to buy horses from the outlying farms. How I wish I had listened to Serel and taken horses with us from Andergarth. We would not have needed the mercenaries to help carry supplies. I had hoped they would also give us added manpower on the road. Once again, my captain was proved right, Devagan and his troop had turned out to be a hindrance rather than a help. My fear that the horses would be seen on the road would have been nothing compared to the trouble the mercenaries have given me.

The witching hour approaches and my small band of seven men are ready. We will leave our campfire burning. Devagan and his savages are sleeping beside their fire a few hundred yards away. Hopefully, it will be dawn before they realise, we have gone. I wanted to leave payment for them in the hope they would turn back home to Andergarth. Serel talked me out of it and of course, he is correct. We will need the money to purchase supplies now that we are abandoning the stuff the Seabloods were supposed to carry for us. I wonder if Serel made this plea as an act of revenge against the hated Devagan. I fear it will backfire on us if they give chase and surely, they will. What have they got to lose? Our only hope is to get as far into the borderlands and then lose them once we hit the Northern frost. The further we go the more we will find Iceblood homesteads and maybe some help.

(Day 8)

It is late afternoon and the light has yet to fade completely. The surrounding land has become rocky, small treeless windswept hills with little shelter. We have made a clearing in a thick patch of wild gorse bushes. This will give us added shelter as well as keep the glow of our campfires at least partially hidden. I finally agreed to take a good night's rest after three days of forced marching. By my reckoning, we have put at least 70 miles between us and the place we left the Seabloods behind. Even if they follow, I am sure we are well enough ahead. They are a ragged bunch and will surely take time to rape and pillage as they move along.

We can only be 150 miles out from the walled city and yet the land could not be more different. Gone are the small villages and the few farms we pass look desolate. The green fields ripe with crops have been replaced by bare moorland. We skirted around a few isolated hovels and have not seen another soul on the road in the last three days. Incredibly we still have 250 miles to go before the true Northern Frost border. Who knows how much further after that until we approach the ruins of Blackbarron. Tomorrow we will have to find habitation and buy supplies. I have underestimated how poor and bleak the land is as we move North. We may not get many more opportunities to procure food never mind horses.

Dawn is breaking and we are almost set to leave camp. Luck was on our side last night. We were all so exhausted that we slept and let the fire burn out. Halfway through the night, I was awakened by Serel. 'My lord, keep quiet, say nothing.' At first, I feared that the Ice Ghosts had infiltrated our camp as the blaze died. We could hear the hooves of multiple horses passing and voices. It was difficult to estimate how many, but we reckoned at least 50. It had to be the Rowallan guard from Andergarth sent to track us down. No doubt the word of Devagan's misdeeds had got back to the walled city and justice was now being demanded. I wonder if they found the mercenaries first. No doubt like all Seabloods they will stick together, and we will be blamed for the murders. I have made my decision; we have no choice. We must find a farm and hope it is owned by Iceblood kin. We need to hide and rebuild our strength for a few days.

We cannot move North until the posse passes us going back South.

(Day 10)

A fire burns brightly in the hearth of the old stone cottage. We have been here for two days, tomorrow we will leave and hope the Rowallan troops have already crossed our path on their way back to Andergarth. The men seem contented, Serel is happier now that we have left Devagan and his band behind. This little farm has gifted us with supplies and even an old donkey who we plan to take with us to carry our packs. We have christened him Borell as that was the name inscribed on the wooden post leading to the farm.

I hated having to agree to the murder of the old peasants who occupied this poor settlement. We tried to reason with them, but they had us down as Iceblood looters who had come to steal and kill. How unfortunate that we should find a loyal Seablood homestead this far North. The old man attacked with his rusty sword even though I pleaded with him. Ankar, the youngest of our troop was the one to cut him down. Sadly, the old woman became hysterical. I shall spare myself having to write about her end. It was wrong,

I know that. The farm has supplies so that means others must visit. As soon as we left the old man would have raised the alarm and with the posse searching for us it would have been the end. We buried the bodies half a mile away on the moor. Hopefully, by the time anyone works out what happened, we will be too far North to be caught.

Already too many have died. How many more before we reach Blackbarron? How many more will die if we find that Blackbarron does not exist? the Ice Ghosts will be waiting to exploit any failure. I know I am leading my small band of followers to certain death but whether we go North or South, the outcome will now be the same.

(Day 12)

Progress was slow over the last two days since we left the farm. Every creeping step forward on the bleak exposed moor brought the inherent danger of us coming face to face with the soldiers of Andergarth. Our new companion Borell the donkey has lightened our load, but it comes at a price. The animal refuses to go at any pace other than a slow amble. No amount of prodding and pushing can convince the beast to increase its speed. By now I had hoped we could have been at least 250 miles closer to Blackbarron, but the unplanned stop means we have barely managed 180.

Dusk was approaching today when we saw the forest. Could this be the first sign that we are nearing the true border country? Trees would be a welcome break from the endless exposed moorland. Once the conifers surround you it is easier to disappear. It is also easier to be ambushed, the landscape can be an enemy as well as an ally. It turned out to be a small wood although a smattering of trees here and there gave the impression of a gradual change in the landscape. Flecks of ice-cold snow filtered through the damp air as we approached. It was Ankar who noticed first, maybe his eyes are sharper with him being the youngest. 'Captain Serel, I see something in the trees.' We all stopped and peered through the gloom.

'My lord, he is right. There is something at the edge of the forest. It does not look right; the shade looks different.' Serel and the men looked at me, waiting for a decision.

'We have no choice. Whatever it is, we have to pass it. Move on but tread slowly until we know for sure what lies in wait for us.'

Tonight, we are camped inside the little forest. The freezing temperature and the first sign of snow mean we must keep at least two fires burning. It is a massive risk if the Andergarth troops are still around but without fire, we will either freeze or meet our first Ice Ghosts. Maybe we are not close enough yet to The Northern Frost, but the floating dead have been seen this far South. Some even speak of seeing them near the walled city in the depths of winter. I know it is just Seablood superstition and old wives' tales, but we are 180 miles out, the Ice Ghosts are now on our doorstep.

At least one threat has disappeared from our horizon. The dark shapes we saw at the edge of the forest was Devagan and his men. All of them stone dead and hanging from the trees. Each one of them strung up in a line, their white faces and bulging eyes mocking us even in death. So, much for Seabloods sticking together. If that is what the posse will do to their own, then I dread to think what justice they might administer to us. I hope and pray the swinging bodies have been left to warn us that we need to keep going North. One thing is for sure, the death sentence has been passed if we dare turn back.

(Day 15)

Just over two weeks since we left Andergarth and finally our luck has turned. Over the last three days, we managed to walk 75 miles through the changing landscape. The moorland has been replaced by craggy outcrops of rock and fir trees as we gain more height. Even Borell seemed to rise to the challenge and accept that he either speed up or be left behind in the wilderness. Yesterday we struck back onto a well-worn path. By now we had accepted that the Andergarth soldiers had either returned to the walled city or we would meet them and die.

I had always hoped to buy supplies from isolated farms and cottages before we hit the border with The Northern Frost. Yet another of the plans we discussed for months in The Walled City has proven to be worthless. Yesterday we arrived at the edge of the Iceblood stronghold of Bentathka. It is the last settlement of any significance this far North. I had always planned to bypass it. Even though it is mostly populated by my race, it has a reputation for being wild and lawless. And yet, here I sit in the house of the First Baron of Bentathka. They knew we were coming, the Andergarth posse had been here a few days before. There was no battle, the posse was 100 strong and could have ransacked the town. The purpose of the visit was simply to warn me. If I did not cross the border and head deep into The Northern Frost, they would be back. I also learned of my sister Kar denouncing her bloodline and turning to Seablood. It seems a law will soon be passed that all Iceblood in the walled city must do the same or leave for the frozen lands.

The Baron has not directly acknowledged my place as the Lord of the Iceblood, but he will help me on my journey to find Blackbarron. I can tell that he wants me gone. The scattered Iceblood race of the borderlands would have little chance if they rallied around there one last King to challenge The Walled City. He will support our journey if only to ease his conscience. I know he expects us to perish from either the cold or the Ice Ghosts.

We are to be supplied with good horses and three scouts who will lead us to the border, 140 miles distant. From that point, we are on our own. I asked my host and others if there had been any sighting of Blackbarron Castle in recent years. The last known information came from two survivors of a party of ten who went in search of it more than eighty years ago. They did not have happy tales to tell of the Northern wastes, but they did say they had seen the ruin. The story goes that they tried everything to break in, but the walls and ramparts refused them entry every time. They eventually attempted to return to Bentathka, but many succumbed to the Ice hosts on the way back. The Baron laughed when he told me of the rumour of a long-lost black key being the only means of entry. 'Fucking old wives tales my Lord, superstition, and nonsense. I am sure that if and when you find it, you will be able to break in.' Even as he spoke, I could feel the black key against my chest, secured by its gold chain.

(Day 17)

After the warm fires and congenial hosts of Bentathka, it felt strange to be back on the road today. One of our seven, Gahor asked Serel if he could stay behind. It was a test of wills. If his request had been granted, then the others may also have tried to back out. Serel did not draw his sword, he did not need to. His words made it plain. 'If you do not follow your King as you are sworn to do, then death will come sooner rather than later. The Baron of this town will either hang you first or wait until the soldiers of Andergarth return to do the same.' Serel edged within inches of Gahor.

'Let me make it plain to you. Let me make it plain to all of you. We are the walking dead; our sentence has already been passed. We have only one task to complete before we die and that is to follow our King to Blackbarron. Do I make myself clear?'

We aim to be at the border within three days. The stout horses and our guides will drive us on to make 50 miles per day. We handed Borell over to a peasant family as a gift before we left. The land grows colder and higher. Rolling hills surround us, covered in trees and the first signs of hard snow. The Bentathka Icebloods led us to some small run-down wooden huts hidden in the trees. A healthy stock of firewood was piled nearby and very soon we had three fires burning, keeping us warm as well as safe. Once the night set in the cold frost descended. The men were silent before drifting off to sleep. We kept watch to make sure the fires continued to roar. No one dare talk about it but now there could be little doubt that the Ice Ghosts floated nearby. Watching and waiting for a chance to freeze our blood.

(Day 20)

By early afternoon we stood at the border with The

Northern Frost. The land ahead looked the same as that behind us. Hills covered with snow and endless trees. And yet, in the far distance, it was possible to make out the line of mountains known as, The Rise of the Dead. The scouts did not stay long. They wished us luck while eyeing us with pity. We are on our own again. We might not see another human being between here and the place we seek. It is not true despite what the people of Andergarth would have you believe. Some wild tribes still roam the Northern Frost, distant long forgotten ancestors of the Iceblood race. Maybe we will meet them, maybe not. One thing is for sure, the Ice Ghosts will watch our every step from here on. Waiting in the shadows, shifting in the dark. Looking for a way through the fire.

(Day 23)

How cold can this land be? Who could live here and survive? It is still more than two weeks before the freeze descends, and the Northern land is ruled by the Ice Ghosts. If we do not find Blackbarron before then we will need to build a camp and surround ourselves with fire. That will be our only hope of surviving the fifty days of black until the sun rises once more. I know now that we will not make it. I probably always knew buy my destiny was set from the day I was born.

Failure has descended on us again. Since crossing the border, we made good progress for two days. The mountains could be seen clearly yesterday as we camped in a clearing on the side of a hill. The men gathered as much loose wood as possible. The horses have to be tethered inside the ring of fire. The Ice Ghosts will not touch them, but the beasts can die of fear if the floating ones come near.

Serel blames himself for letting the men slacken off but, in all honesty, every one of us became too relaxed. The big mistake was to leave only one guard on watch while the rest of us slept. The ear-piercing scream of death woke us in the black hours. At first, there was confusion, but one thing was clear. One of the fires was almost out and the other two were dying. We then realised that the floating death was upon us, and everyone raced to rebuild the flames. Serel lifted a burning torch to hold the camp while the rest of us fanned the fires and added fuel. We found the watch, frozen and dead. It was young Ankar, he had fallen asleep. Once the fire nearest to him died, the icy touch of death froze his blood. His last scream saved us all from the same fate.

Today we made solemn heavy progress through the increasingly rocky landscape. Snow now falls hard, and the horses are having difficulty keeping their feet. Serel looked at me and we both knew that very soon we would have to abandon the beasts and go on foot. Four fires are burning as the sharp black descends. No one will sleep tonight; the wind is moaning through the trees behind us while the fires flicker in wilting defiance. The shape of death floats around us at the edge of the camp, watching and waiting to add six more to the frost.

(Day 25)

Much has occurred during the last two days of our journey into hell. I no longer care if we live or die. It is only a matter of time before our end comes. Yesterday we made very slow progress through the loose rock and snow as the ground continued to rise upwards. Gatak's horse was the first to fall, taking him with it into the soft snow. I told the men to dismount and abandon the horses. It was Gahor who answered, 'Lord Blackbarron, we go no further.' The revolt was on. The other three soldiers moved over to stand with him. Serel stood with his hand on the hilt of his sword a short distance from the men. He replied first.

'You will do as ordered or die here in the snow.' The four men stood firm as Gahor stared his Captain down.

'Draw your sword as you will Serel. We go no further, you will have to kill all four of us.' For a while, the group stood still in the swirling wind and snow. No one spoke but some distance away we could hear the mournful howling of the snow wolves. Maybe they sensed our end was nigh and hoped to get to us first, before the Ice Ghosts gathered. It was my turn to speak.

'You can all go whichever way you wish. We shall split the rations in six ways. Those going back can take the horses. I wish you all good luck although I fear none of us will have any.' Serel walked over to my side as I spoke. Only two of us would be continuing North.

Today Serel and I hiked further through the Mountains as the driving snow and cold gnawed at our bodies. Ahead of us, it looks to be an impossible climb over The Rise of The Dead. A towering range of white peaks that stare down at us. We have a small fire going, maybe it will not be enough to keep them at bay. The howling of the snow wolves means they are near. Tonight, it may well be the Ice Ghosts who will find us first, and then we can leave this frozen world at last.

As I write what I expect to be my last entry into this journal, Serel is speaking and pointing. Are we delirious? In the distance through the blizzard is a light. It looks to be another fire. Now that I focus, I can see other yellow lights flickering. There is more than one fire burning. Someone else is alive in this frozen white hell.

(Day 27)

Once again good fortune has fallen at our feet. The Rathkan tribe is a squalid troop of Iceblood nomads. They accepted us into their meagre village of winter huts but only because we offered to pay. There chief, Lozak says the right words but his eyes show distrust and cruelty. They are no doubt long lost ancestors of the Iceblood kin, but they do not care for me or my search for Blackbarron. The Rathkan lives in two settlements, one North of The Rise of The Dead mountains and this one. They migrate here in readiness for the coming fifty days of black. It does not bode well that such a hardy group of people cannot survive the onslaught of the dark nights. This is the land that both I and Serel will leave for in the morning. I sense that Lozak sees an opportunity for himself in our deadly journey.

There are six decrepit huts, each with a fire burning both inside and at the door. This is the only guarantee the nomads have that they will not be touched by the floating ones. I cannot be sure, but it looks like they are about thirty strong, including women and brats. It is hard to tell between the sexes; they are all filthy with long straggling hair and cracked dirty faces. Lozak gave us our own hut and his people kept the fires burning and supplied us with food. It was a chance to recharge and regain our strength but Serel hardly slept. He did not trust the tribe; I know he expects them to murder us in our sleep and take the last of our gold. We intend to leave before the sun rises and be away from the Rathkan before they awake.

(Day 28)

As I write this at the end of the fourth week of our journey, I begin to wonder if destiny walks in my shadow. We have either had an incredible stroke of luck or this is another trick being played out on us before the Cold finally consumes our diminished party. As we crept away from Lozak and his people in the grey dawn we became aware that we were being followed. The meagre sun was rising in the distance with little sign of yesterday's snow. It remained well below freezing.

It was Serel who sensed it first. 'My Lord, someone is behind us, I am sure of it.' We ran forward to make tracks in the snow and then doubled back a few hundred yards and waited in the trees. Within five minutes a lone figure covered in animal fur came shuffling along in our footprints. Serel waited until he had passed to make sure others did not follow. Once he was assured that the stranger was alone, he drew his sword and pounced. Within seconds he was on the intruder and dragged him to the ground. The steel glinted in the low morning sun as he raised it to make the kill.

'Stop Serel. Wait, wait. We have nothing to lose in asking why he is following.' Serel had the bloodlust in his eyes as he replied.

'The filthy Rathkan scum follows to murder us. Why the fuck else would they sneak along like rats in our tracks?' He pulled his victim around in the snow and poked the end of the sword in the snow-covered face.

'Speak, speak now and convince me why I should not cut your filthy body in two. Why did you follow us, speak scum, speak?' By now I was beside Serel and held my arm up to push his sword away before he administered the execution.

'It is a fucking woman Serel. Hold your sword. At least let her answer.' Even though she was covered in filthy furs and her face was lined with dirt, I could make out she was young. Probably in her early twenties but no older.

'Who are you? Tell me before I let my Captain finish you off, girl.' It was not the name she gave that took us by surprise but what she said after that.

'My name is Jahvelia, I am one of Lozak's eleven children. I follow you because like me you are running away from him. He planned to murder you before you left. They would have made a leaving breakfast and then beheaded both of you while you ate.' Serel looked at me and shook his head.

'We need to kill her Lord. This is bullshit, they will certainly follow and more so now if she is here.' I held my arm up to quieten him before continuing to question her.

'Why do you follow us? We cannot help you escape your father. We are going to a certain death. That is our destiny, but you can live, if you return.' Serel became angry at my response.

'Lord, she will have them on us. We cannot let her go back. We need to kill her and get out of here before that bastard Lozak comes after us.' Jahvelia turned to face Serel with steel cold eyes.

'Such a brave man who administers death with ease.' She turned her attention to me before going on.

'If I go back, I will die and so will you two. If we go on together then we might all live.'

'And why is that, tell me, girl?'

'Because I have seen Blackbarron. I know the way to find it, through the mountains of The Rise of The Dead. Take me with you to free me from him and I will free you.'

(Day 33)

The last five days have taken us to the very depths of this frozen hell. Our guide Jahvelia has so far been true to her word. We have clamoured, climbed and crawled our way through narrow mountain passages thick with snow. We fall and curse every step in the ice-filled waste. The Rise of The Dead tower above us from every side and yet the young woman seems to find a way through without us having to scale the impossible cloud-covered peaks. We have taken risks and continued until the night is truly upon us. As soon as we sense the Ice hosts are near, we camp and light a fire.

Trees and scrub to burn are becoming harder to find. Each of us carries as much as we can lift during the days march.

Serel and Jahvelia look at each other with hatred and distrust. And yet, I trust her because she needs us as much as we need her. No doubt death awaits at the hands of her father if she returns. Maybe she already suffered a fate worse than death while she lived with the Rathkan. She says little and will only answer questions with persuasion. In her words, Blackbarron stands but is impenetrable to all. The Rathkan are afraid of it, they believe it is the home of the Ice Ghosts. I have told her that it will be our only hope of refuge when the black descends. I find it strange that she never asks how we intend to get inside.

Jahvelia reckons we have two more days until we reach my ancestral home. That will only leave five days before the winter falls. At that point, the only way to survive the fifty days of black will be to let the fires burn brightly. We will only have those few days to find wood and food to keep us alive. Without fire, even a castle will fall prey to the floating ones.

I watch Serel sitting opposite me. His grey beard covered in frost, every line in his face tells a story of death. Without his undying loyalty, I would not have got this far.

And yet, maybe his loyalty is the reason so many have died. I know I would not have made it more than a few days out of Andergarth if he had not been by my side.

Tomorrow we face our biggest challenge yet. The girl tells me that there is nothing but rocks and snow between here and the forest of Blackbarron. It will be a race against time, and we will only have fuel for one night's fire. If we do not find the castle by the day after tomorrow, then the Ice Ghosts will have us.

(Day 34)

I am sure this will be the last words I write in this journal. I now truly hope it is and that my end will arrive when the sun rises tomorrow. I sit huddled around the tiny fire with Jahvelia. Even though we are wrapped in furs the cold still gnaws at my body. Serel is dead. Now he has joined the 19 who set out with me 34 days ago. All are in the grave and it is my fault. This was a futile journey, one driven by my pride. I could have stayed in Andergarth and played the game, even denounced my Iceblood heritage and taken the Seablood vow. It is all too late now.

It was not long after we broke camp this morning that

we realised that Lozak and his Rathkan tribe were hunting us down. It was Jahvelia who sensed it and soon we could see the dots moving across the snow in the distance behind us. They were at least ten strong, we had no chance of fighting it out. 'We need to leave the girl, my lord. Leave her for them or they will surely catch us.'

'How do we leave her Serel? She will just follow us anyway.' He looked at me, for once his patience was gone.

'For fuck sake Lord Blackbarron. We bind her, so she cannot move until they find her.' I did not need to answer. It was Jahvelia who walked within a few feet of Serel, her eyes piercing deep into his.

'They are not following me you fucking sword-wielding halfwit. It is him they want.' They both turned to look at me.

'Why do they want him, bitch? You will say anything to save your stinking hide and hand us to your father.' Jahvelia laughed and I could see Serel's hand moving towards his sword, ready to strike her down whether I ordered it or not.

'My father knows you must have the secret to Blackbarron. Why else would you be going there when no one else has ever been able to get inside.' She had hardly spoken the words as Serel raised his arm to bring his sword down to carve her head in two.

I had no choice. No that is not true, I did have a choice and, in that split, second, I made my decision. I can still see his eyes, frozen like a black lake. Boring through me and yet even in death, he honoured my call. His last words, 'My Lord' uttered even as his body crumpled into the ice. His deep red blood merging with the frozen snow. I pulled my sword from his chest and we both turned towards the North. The ice shall be his grave.

As I go to place my scribe down, Jahvelia places her hand on my arm. Neither of us understands why she is the one who still lives and not him. Does it matter? Death comes to us all, it is only the order that is debatable.

(The Ice Ghosts shall have their night)

Lozak looked down at the body. Already the blood had frozen hard into the snow. His tribe stood around him, their eyes filled with fear, desperation in their hearts. Why did their chief not speak? The men already knew that it was too late to turn back. The fall of the dark was only five days away. It was now past the point of return. Their only hope was to catch the girl and the southerners. And yet, they did not understand why Lozak had driven them back North.

And now he looked uncertain as he stared at the body. He was never unsure, he administered death and decisions with precision and ease. It was Skalrog who dared speak first. 'Lozak, what shall we do? It will be dark soon and we have not collected fire.' The words jerked Lozak out of his trance.

'Shut fucking up Skalrog or you will feel my blade on your throat. We continue north after them.' The men looked unhappy and at first, it seemed they might not follow but once Lozak had taken a few steps they started to shuffle after him.

The ragged group marched through the biting wind and snow until the sun disappeared and the black cold ate into their souls. Lozak was still lost in his thoughts. He had expected it to be his daughter lying dead in the snow. The fact it was one of the southerners confused him. He was always correct in his assumptions and yet this time he was wrong. Maybe it was the sight of Serel's dead body that caused him to make the wrong decision. Lozak was so caught up in his determination to hunt down his prey that it was only now dawning on him. The night was already well and truly upon them. He stopped and turned around to face the men. He could see the blind terror in their eyes. 'Make camp, make camp, quick get the fires burning.'

But it was already too late. They all knew it as soon as

the first blood-curdling scream pierced through the frozen air. For the first time in his life, even Lozak knew fear. The Ice Ghosts were upon them. The men ran in different directions, their eyes bulging in despair. It was no use, each and everyone one of them fell like blocks of frozen stone as the floating ones touched them. The last to go was Lozak, his sword drawn in a hopeless last stand. The white shape simply glided towards him and with one touch he became another dead body in the surrounding white wasteland.

Ten miles in the distance the Greystone walls of the magnificent ancient castle of Blackbarron stood proud in the surrounding forest. The massive Iron entrance sealed tightly against all intruders. At least fifty barred windows stared down from an impressive height at the frozen landscape below. Within five days the black would fall and the only thing that would move would be the floating white shapes of death. And yet even the souls of the dead would not be allowed to penetrate these thick stone walls. Even more so now as two of the windows no longer held a deep dark shadow. Instead, the glow of orange flames could be seen flickering behind the bars. Life had returned after more than 200 years. At last, the living for once outnumbered the dead in the Northern Frost. Well, at least it did in the Castle of Blackbarron.

The Path by Richard M Pearson

On a path filled with ghosts and secrets, nobody is safe.

For neurotic Ralph and easy-going Harvey, the trek across the remote, rolling hills of Scotland is a chance to get away from life, an opportunity to rediscover their place in the world. At least that's the plan. But they are two middle-aged, unfit men trying to cross one hundred miles of rugged terrain.

Despite that, they might have had a chance if that was their only problem. Unfortunately, not only are they alcoholics, someone or something is stalking them, watching their every move. Worse, one man carries a terrible secret about why he went on the trip. A secret that will turn a friendly trek into something far darker. It's a safe bet that if either man survives, he will never be the same again.

The Path is the first novel by Richard M Pearson. A gothic ghost story for modern times that builds up an atmosphere of foreboding and fear.

(Amazon review)

A terrific read. I thoroughly enjoyed this novel. Atmospheric, melancholic, laced with pathos and wry humour. Excellent plot and an intriguing outcome. Strong characterisation, complex and endearing personas, more so for their flaws and imperfections. The poems were also a nice touch. Almost offering a staging post for the author's state of mind as each chapter ends. I can highly recommend The Path, it won't disappoint.

(Available from Amazon)

RICHARD M PEARSON

THE PATH

A GHOST STORY?

Deadwater by Richard M Pearson

Who would dare to unlock the secret of Deadwater Mansion?

It is only when you look back at things from the distance of many years that you finally understand why. The problem was we in the village blamed the aristocratic Denham-Granger family for our bad fortune. Everything was their fault according to us but in hindsight, that was more to do with jealousy than reality. We hated them because they had wealth and looked down on us as uneducated peasants.

But the truth was, they were as much victims as we were. No, the real holder of all the power through the years was Deadwater. The grand three-story country mansion cast its shadow over the village and manipulated everything to survive. So, when it realised that time was running out it played the final card, and then dark retribution crawled out of that room to hunt each of its victims down.

Deadwater, A Classic Gothic Ghost Story with a shocking twist.

(Available from Amazon)

FROM THE AUTHOR OF 'THE PATH'

RICHARD M
PEARSON

DEADWATER

WHO CAN FREE THE SECRET OF DEADWATER HOUSE?

Broken Leaves by Richard M Pearson

Only she knows the terrible secret of his past.

A dark thriller to keep you reading through the night.

One moment of madness in his youth has caught up with Matt Cunningham. The only person who can save the successful business executive is his alcoholic ex-lover Roni Paterson. But how do you find a woman who has disappeared for thirty years and what if she becomes part of the unfolding nightmare?

Blackmail, Murder, Love, Hate. There is nowhere left to hide when revenge comes calling.

(Amazon review)

I cannot recommend this book highly enough. Thoroughly enjoyed it and could not put it down from the minute I started it. The plot kept me guessing until the end and the characterisations were fantastic. Such a believable story and so well written. Five stars. This is the third book I have read by this author so if you're looking for an excellent read, I would recommend this along with The Path and Deadwater.

(Available from Amazon)

BROKEN

THERE IS NOWHERE LEFT TO HIDE

LEA∨ES

WHEN REVENGE COMES CALLING

RICHARD M PEARSON

Printed in Great Britain
by Amazon